A WITCH, HER CAT AND THE DEVIL DOGS
A tale of a Scarborough Witch, her Cat, and Evil on the North Yorkshire Moors

By Graham Rhodes

First published 2016
Internet Kindle Edition 2016

Templar Publishing Scarborough N. Yorkshire
Copyright G. A. Rhodes 2016

Conditions of Sale.

This book is sold subject to the condition that it shall not, by way of trade or otherwise, be lent, re-sold, hired out, or otherwise circulated without the publishers prior consent, in any form of binding or cover other than that in which it is published.

All rights reserved. No part of this publication may be reproduced, stored in a retrieval system, or transmitted, in any form or by any means, electronic, mechanical, photocopying, recording or otherwise, without the prior permission of the publishers and copyright holder.

Also available in the series Agnes the Scarborough Witch -

A Witch, Her Cat and a Pirate:
A story of a Scarborough Witch, her Cat and John Paul Jones

A Witch, her Cat and the Ship Wreckers
A story of a Scarborough witch, her cat and ship wreckers and highwaymen.

Dedication

This is the third book of Agnes. As usual it would have been impossible without the help and encouragement of the following people –

Yvonne, Jesse, Frankie & Heather (& Granddad), Richard, Chris, The Badgers Of Bohemia, Jo, Tubbs & Missy, Lucy, Magenta, Anna (Whose Gig At The SJT Started all this off) & all at Cellars, Dennis & Dave, and finally Ysanne in the hope that one day it will turn up in her bookshop.

Many of the streets and places mentioned in this book still exist in Scarborough's old town and up on the moors. They are well worth visiting. Once again I have taken the liberty of using the names of old Scarborough fishing families. I hope they don't mind their ancestors appearing here. However the names and characters are all fictitious and should not be confused with anyone living or dead.

Character List

Agnes 21st & 18th Centuries
Our hero, an elderly lady who, as far as she knows, is over three hundred years old. She has no memory of who she is or where she came from. She lives in the same cottage in the Old Town of Scarborough in both centuries. She is either a wize woman or a witch, depending on who is telling the story. She is also a computer hacker.

Marmaduke 21st & 18th Centuries
Marmaduke lives with Agnes in her cottage. In the 21st century he is an old, grumpy, one eared, one eyed, sardine addicted cat. In the 17th century he is a one eyed one eared six foot high ex-highwayman with very dangerous habits.

Andrew Marks 18th Century
The proprietor of the Chandlery situated on Scarborough's 17th century harbourside. Andrew is the eyes and ears of the small port. Nothing comes or goes in or out the port without him knowing about it, either legal or illegal.

The Garrison Commander 18th Century
The military commander of the Garrison based at Scarborough's Castle. Posted to Scarborough for a mistake he made during the American of Independence he is very definitely a soldier of the old school.

Lieutenant Smalls
A young military man and the right hand man of the Garrison Commander. An intelligent and thoughtful officer who could go far.

Whitby John
Ex-fisherman and landlord of The Three Mariners, Agnes's favourite public house.

Salmon Martin
A fisherman and regular of the Three Mariners.

Old Sam
A storyteller and drinker

Mathew Tong
Drinker

Baccy Lad
A young lad eager to please and helper at the Three Mariners

Joan
A farmer's widow.

Peter
A very fortunate shepherd

Emma
A fortunate shepherds wife

Boggles
Enough said!

Mrs Pateley
The new broom that sweeps the Three Mariners

The Man in Black with Red Eyes
A very bad man

A Captain & His First Mate
Chancers!

Nostaa Demonit
A Finnish Death Metal Band

Tapio Lillmans
A Finnish Death Metal Singer & lyricist

Young Man (Death Metal musician)
A very helpful ex-member of Nostaa Demonit

A WITCH, HER CAT AND THE DEVIL DOGS

Chapter One

The snow had been falling for almost a week now. It had closed all the roads leading into the small coastal town. The road south was closed by an overturned lorry that had skidded across two lanes of snow and ice covered highway. The road north was blocked by a line of traffic queuing behind a broken down snow plough. The route inland was closed by a cold wind blowing the snow off the tops of the Wolds right across the main road that led to the cities of York and beyond to Leeds.

The traffic news wasn't good. Agnes gave a disapproving sniff and pointed the remote at the television. The room suddenly went silent and dark. She stood up switched on the light and drew the curtains. She nestled down in her chair and pulled a warm wrap around her. She pointed the remote at the television again and flipped through the channels until she reached the radio section. She found the local BBC station and listened as the presenter interviewed various guests, updated the national and local news, and every few minutes gave ever more gloomy weather and traffic reports. It looked like no one was going anywhere, for a while at least. She got up and walked into the kitchen where she opened a cupboard. There were five large packs of cat food, each holding ten individual foil packets. Enough for the best part of a week, more probably. She checked the rest of her kitchen and smiled. She had stocked up on provisions thanks to the supermarkets on-line delivery man. That was another advantage of living in 2014, on-line deliveries. Just don't trust them with fruit and veg. She learnt that after the first delivery. The state that the courgettes and oranges arrived in were beyond even her magic powers of regeneration. She closed the cupboards, glad that there was no urgent need for her to leave the house. At least in 2014.

There was a need for her to venture out in another

time. She had been preparing a special lotion for an old friend, very old. It was Whitby John, whom records showed was the landlord of the Three Mariners public house, in 1799. He'd badly damaged his back whilst trying to prevent a cask of brandy falling off the bar. At least that's what he claimed. In actual fact he had sprained his back muscle trying to get it off the back of a boat that was riding unanchored on a high tide just below the Castle headland, out of sight of the harbour and the customs officers. She opened her fridge and picked up a very small jar of lotion that had been cooling next to the milk. Before she left the kitchen she kicked the cat flap. It opened, allowing Marmaduke her large one-eyed cat access in and out of the house as he pleased. She put the jar in her pocket and walked towards the cellar door. On the way she checked in the front room. It seemed that currently Marmaduke's main pleasure was spending as much time as possible curled up on a cushion in the most comfortable chair in the house. He deigned to open an eye as she left the room. She marched down her cellar steps. Halfway down she turned, stepped through a small door that shouldn't have been there and emerged in 1799. She carefully placed a shawl over her shoulders and stepped out into the narrow cobbled street. A few flickering lights could be seen shining through the gaps in the shutters covering her neighbours windows. She glanced up between the tight little roofs to the small patch of darkening sky overhead. Clouds were forming. She sniffed the air. Fighting through the permanent smell of smoke from coal fires, old fish, damp oiled wool and the contents of the old towns earth closets she could just make out the cold smell of approaching snow. She pulled her shawl tighter around her shoulders. Times may change, but the weather always remained constant.

As she walked into the Three Mariners she stopped and blinked. That was usual as the eyes always took a few seconds to adjust when entering into the gloomy, smoke filled, beer stained atmosphere. What was unusual was that she was forced to blink again, in order to take in the sight that presented itself to her. The body of a man was hanging upside down from the rafters. A loop of rope was around his ankles and was tied around the ancient oak beam. The building was low so that the unfortunate man's head just brushed the dirt and old straw that covered the stone-flagged floor. Instinctively she lifted her hand and began to form a spell of protection. A voice sounded out.

"Steady on, Agnes. It's alright, really."

It was a voice she recognised, it was the voice of Salmon Martin a local fisherman, so named not because of the fish he caught, but because of an unfortunate shaped mouth that drooped at the sides and gave him the appearance of a fish that had just been hooked. She looked closer at the figure hanging upside down. Now her eyes had adjusted to the gloom she recognised the man as Whitby John, the landlord.

Before she could say anything another voice piped up out of the gloom.

"It's to stretch him, to make his back better."

Another voice from the back of bar added, "An old captain I sailed with used to swear by it!"

She bent down to have a closer look. Even in the gloom she could see that Whitby Johns face was turning a horrible shade of purple. She turned to the rest of the occupants of the bar.

"For Gods sake get him down. The bloods rushing to his head, He'll pass out in a minute."

There was a murmur of disapproval. A voice deep in the darkness muttered "Bloody woman coming in spoiling our fun."

She whipped round to face the speaker. "Mathew Tong, if I suspected you had a brain in that head of yours I'd be tempted to batter some sense into it. Get him down before he bursts a blood vessel. If that happens there will be no one to open up the inn, and you'll all have to drink in the Beehive."

That threat of drinking in the Beehive worked better than the threat of violence. Violence was what the fishermen understood. They faced it everyday, the violence of the sea and the weather, the violence of the Customs Officers, the violence of the press gangs, the violence of poverty and disease. They understood violence; they accepted it as part of their lives. What they couldn't understand was how the landlord of the Beehive contrived to ruin every barrel of beer he touched. Beer could enter the Beehive inn as tasty and as bitter and sweet as any beer in the county but somehow, when the landlord poured it out of the spigots and taps, it tasted as if every cat in the neighbourhood had used the barrel as a urinal.

A couple of men stood up and released the

landlord's feet by cutting the rope. He fell to the ground in a mass of arms and legs. A loud groan came out of his mouth. After a deal of pushing and pulling and huffing and puffing they eventually got him sitting upright in a chair.

Agnes looked at the men standing around her. "Whose idea was this?"

Salmon Martin spoke up for the rest of them. "We thought stretching would be good for his back."

Agnes shook her head. "I can understand that bit. What I don't understand is why upside down?"

When she asked that question Agnes noticed that they all looked a bit sheepish, she was picking up certain fission in the air. At the back of the bar someone sniggered. Then the penny dropped.

She nodded gravely at the assembly. "Do I take it that there is a hitherto unknown benefit of treating a person who is hanging upside down?"

The snigger turned into a loud guffaw, the guffaw turned into laughter, the laughter was infectious. It spread until the only two people in the bar that weren't laughing were the landlord and Agnes. Even then Agnes found that she was fighting a loosing battle to stifle a grin.

Whitby John however was definitely not amused. "Do you mean you had me hanging upside down just to amuse yourselves?" he spluttered when he could actually speak.

A variety of voices clamoured out in their self-defence.

"You were thinking it was doing you good!"

"You said you could feel it doing you good!"

"Beneficial you said. I heard you!"

Whitby John staggered to his feet. "Right – Out the lot of you. Out right now. The bars closed. I… Owwwww!"

He sank back into the chair quicker than he had risen out of it. Agnes could see the proposed stretching cure hadn't worked. She placed her bottle of lotion on the counter.

"Right! John rub that on your back, first thing in the morning and last thing at night!"

Whitby John glared at her but slide the small bottle into his pocket. The rest of the bars occupants weren't that happy to be thrown out into the night. Many of them hadn't finished their drinks, it was cold outside and it looked as if it would snow soon. They began to murmur and argue among themselves. Agnes could tell that a fight was about to erupt. It was a familiar feeling as nearly every night a fight broke out about something. The occasional nights it didn't break out because of something, it tended to break out because of nothing. Agnes grew weary of it and tonight she decided to do something about it. She stepped behind the bar and reached underneath for the belay pin she knew John kept there. As the noise and arguments grew she dragged the wooden pin out into sight and slammed it onto the top of the bar. There was silence.

"Right! John, you're taking to your bed. Don't argue. I'll look after the bar until closing time. Then I'll lock up. Rub that lotion on and you and your back will be better in the morning."

Whitby John opened his mouth to say something, than saw the look on Agnes' face and thought better of it. He leant across the bar and took a bottle of brandy from the shelf and shuffled through the door that led upstairs. There were a few moments of silence as everyone listened to the sound of Johns footsteps clumping up the wooden steps. They all remained silent and watched the ceiling as they listened to the sound of his feet shuffling across the floor above their head. Then there was a silence followed by a loud thud and a distant groan. He'd made it onto his bed. As if it were some sort of secret sign everyone started talking at once and they all stepped forward to the bar holding out various mugs and tankards and all demanding to be served first. Agnes hit the top of the bar with the belay pin once again and demanded they form an orderly queue. Getting in line was an unusual concept for the fishermen, getting in an orderly line was unique. Eventually after a lot of murmurs and grumbles and elbow nudges everyone was served and they all drifted back to their respective seats, the entertainment was over for the night. Around the room small pockets of conversation sprung up and the public bar returned to what everyone considered normal.

As evenings went it proved to be an enjoyable

night. It did Agnes good to be out and about and enjoy a normal conversation about ordinary things with normal people. In the Old Town everyone knew Agnes, and knew the contribution she made to their community. They accepted her and she accepted them on the same level.

Eventually the conversation drifted, as it always did, to the fishing. She discovered the rough seas and high tides had prevented anyone from putting to sea for the last three days now. That explained the tetchiness in the inn. It meant that most people in the Old Town weren't earning which was always a worry. If the boats didn't bring in the fish there was nothing for the women to gut, no need for them to bait the lines. If there was no fish there was no market and the merchants spent their cash elsewhere. If there was no money coming in the shops didn't sell their goods. Pretty soon without the fishing the economy of the entire Old Town faltered. It meant that worries increased and tempers grew short. It meant that everyone spent their time doing small jobs on their boats or around the house, doing the little things that had been put aside for such a rainy day. As they worked they all kept a weather eye open knowing that whatever they were doing, it would all be dropped as soon as the conditions changed and the wind turned.

Baccy Lad, so called because of his habit of chewing tobacco and not, as he was very quick to point out, due to his habit of smuggling tobacco, was propping up the far end of the bar. He had just visited his sister up at Hackness, a small village in a valley set underneath the edge of the moors. He was deep in conversation with Salmon Martin. Agnes edged forward to overhear what was being said.

"Right carry on up there." He was saying. "Seems a couple of sheep got killed. They found them with their throats ripped out. I reckon some sort of wild dogs loose up on the moors, though some of the folk up there reckon it's some sort of devil dog."

Salmon Martin shook his head. "Always some sort of rumour up there. Superstitious lot them folk that live up on the moor."

They were joined by a third man. Old Sam, who had left his comfortable spot by the fire to get his tankard refilled, was drawn towards the conversation after hearing the words Devil Dog. He was a great storyteller and knew all the local legends, especially if there was the chance of a free drink at the end of its telling. If there wasn't a suitable local legend he would make one up to fit the circumstances. In the past he had amazed visitors and locals alike with tales of mermaids seen swimming off Filey Brigg. Ghostly ships with ragged black sails sailing along the Esk out of Whitby Harbour. Strange fairy creatures called Boggles that lived in holes in the cliffs. No one ever believed a word he said, but they all agreed he told a rattling good yarn.

"There's a legend up those parts. The legend of the

Barghest!"

The pub fell silent as everyone turned to listen to Old Sam. They all filled their tankards and settled down to listen to Old Sam tell the story of the Barghest, a monstrous back dog with huge teeth and claws that inhabited the distant moors and roamed the fells and valleys. It was said that one day the dog padded out of the moors and made its home in the City of York where it skulked and stalked through the towns many dark alleys and snickleways, preying on unsuspecting travellers. How it howled at nights and was even seen in the Minster Precinct.

Sam's telling was good and, as he told his tale, even Agnes felt a cold shiver creep down her back.

Eventually the story ended with the giant dog being cornered by a group of local constables, but before they could capture the creature it made a gigantic bound up and over the City Wall and was never seen again. As the story came to an end Agnes called time and everyone began to drift off to their respective homes. Agnes smiled to herself as she noticed they all left in twos and threes. After hearing Old Sam's tale no one left alone, and everyone whether they left in twos or threes, avoided walking along the narrowest of the Old Towns alleyways. She locked the door behind them, and poured herself a Spanish sherry from a bottle she found hidden at the back of the bar and, glass in one hand bottle in the other, walked across to the fire, fully intending to tamp it down for the night. Instead she sat down in a comfortable settle. The warmth from the fire met with the warmth of the sherry from the inside. She found herself closing her eyes and soon she had drifted off to sleep.

She woke up shivering in the early hours. The fire had gone out .Thin grey daylight had forced its way through the grimy windows and was tapping at the front of her forehead. At first she wondered where she was. Then she felt her head throb and she realised that her mouth felt like something had passed by and died in it. There was a stabbing pain in one of her eyes. Upstairs she could hear the snoring of Whitby John. She climbed out of the settle and found a tankard half-full of stale ale on a nearby table. She cast her hand over it and it began to fizz. She lifted it to her lips and drank it back in one long gulp. She felt the liquid go through her body and a feeling of calm run through her veins. Her head stopped throbbing and her bones stopped aching. Her mouth felt refreshed. She put the tankard down with a smile. She hadn't needed her hangover spell for a lot of years now. She walked across to the front door and let herself out. She locked it and slipped the key back under the door. She flicked her fingers to cast a little spell over it. The only person to see the key would be Whitby John and once he touched it the spell would be broken. Well, she thought to herself, you can't be too careful.

Outside the temperature had dropped. The early morning air was crisp, the sky clear and the moon was ringed with a rainbow. Frost was settling on the cobbles making them dance and sparkle, as if someone had dropped a bag of diamonds. Agnes pulled her shawl tighter over her shoulders and walked carefully up the Dog and Duck steps heading home. As she stood opening her front door, a shadow briefly crossed the face of the moon. Agnes felt another shiver pass down her spine but put it down to the frost. She turned around but saw nothing.

Chapter Two

When she woke later in the mid morning she opened her curtains and looked out onto the red roof tiles of the Old Town houses. They were white, inches deep in snow. She got up and threw her dressing gown around her shoulders, went to the kitchen, made a pot of tea and went back to bed. Her bedside radio spluttered into life. As always it was tuned to the local radio station. The weather reports were getting worse. The snow was still falling and more roads were becoming un-passable. Traffic had come to a standstill and trains were being cancelled all over the north of England. It was beginning to look like the winter of 2014 was going to be a bad one. She lay back in her bed and stretched out her legs. Her feet touched something soft and furry. Marmaduke had taken possession of the bottom of her bed.

She tried listening to the radio but felt restless. She sat up, something was bothering her. Something was nagging away at the back of her mind. She closed her eyes and brought to mind her night in the Mariners. She recalled Old Sam's tale of the Barghest and smiled, he'd got it half right. She remembered falling asleep and waking up, she remembered the walk home in the clear crisp late night, early morning air. She saw the frost sparkling on the cobbles and the ring around the moon that hung in a cloudless winter's night. She saw herself opening her front door, something moved. She stopped the vision as if it were a video and rewound it. There it was, a shadow briefly caused by something passing the moon. It couldn't be a cloud, there were no clouds. Perhaps it was an owl, though deep down she doubted it. She washed, dressed, and went downstairs. Marmaduke followed rubbing his body against her legs as she tried to go down the stairs.

"One day you'll have us both down these steps!"

she thought. The cat stopped and twitched its ears as if it heard her thoughts.

Later that morning she decided she'd return to the Three Mariners and check on Whitby John. She knew her medicine was good but wanted to know how good and whether he was up and about. She left Marmaduke curled up in the easy chair. She could tell he was preparing to sleep his way through the bad weather. She stopped and considered it for a moment. Perhaps he'd chosen the right option.

As she opened her door and stepped out into 1779 the cold almost took her breath away. An icy wind was blowing in from the sea bringing with it more than a hint of snow. Icicles hung from the gutters of houses and water butts were frozen. A friendly voice called out to her, telling her to be careful, not to slip. She nodded in the direction it came from. The Dog and Duck steps were particularly slippery and she was grateful to hang onto the rough stonework of the walls of the small houses that lined its route on her way down.

Across from the bottom of the steps, she saw that the door to the Mariners was open. She walked in and was greeted by a roaring fire blazing in the hearth. Whitby John was busy behind the bar wiping and polishing the surface with a cloth that, for its own sake, should have been thrown away years ago. He looked up as she approached the bar.

"Don't suppose you know anything about a bottle of Spanish sherry?" He asked

I wasn't exactly the greeting she'd expected. She looked blank. The landlord pulled an empty bottle out from under the bar. He placed it on the counter between then.

"Found it tucked down the back of the settle this morning!"

Agnes reddened. Oh, that bottle of sherry she thought. She smiled.

"I might have had a nightcap!"

The landlord spluttered and held up the bottle. "Empty!"

Agnes grimaced. Well, she thought to herself, that explains the hangover.

Whitby John leant forward. "I don't mind. Lord knows a bottle of sherry is the least I could give you for what you did last night. The takings were up, you put all the money in the drawer, you even tidied up. It's just that is was a special bottle for a certain lady. I'd promised her it like."

Agnes managed to look shamefaced. "It wouldn't by any chance be for her that lives at the top of Paradise, opposite St Mary's church. Her that lost her husband at sea last year?"

Whitby John stood back. "Problem with you is you know too much!"

Agnes shook her head. "Signs John, I just read the signs!"

"Pity you didn't read the sign on that bottle of sherry!" He muttered.

"I'll pay you for it." She offered.

The landlord leant forward and, despite the fact there were only the two of them in the bar he began to speak in a whisper. "Money's not the problem. The problem is I bought it of a bloke who bought it… well you know what I mean."

He gave a conspiratorial wink. "Anyway I don't know if he's got any left!"

Agnes sighed. Why was life was always so complicated! "When was this?"

"Last week when that shipment of brandy came through."

"Well we all know who to go to…"

The Landlord stepped back. "You might. As far as I'm concerned if the revenue men see me walking in there they'll be all over me like a rash!"

Agnes sighed again. "I'll go. See what I can do."

John placed the bottle in front of Agnes and as he scratched around in his apron she placed it in her pocket. Suddenly John found what he was looking for and pulled out a silver half guinea piece.

"Here, take this, I'll have the bottle but I'll be blowed if you're going to pay for it."

Agnes took the coin. Looked at it and put it in her mouth and bit its edge. She looked at John and winked. They both laughed.

Outside the day wasn't getting any warmer. The wind was still bringing a chill as if it was blowing directly from the arctic into the harbour mouth. Along the cobbled pavement some publicans and shop-keepers had spread sawdust to help keep everyone on their feet. Agnes managed to stagger around the corner and down a narrow lane. She emerged by the Chandlery on the front of the harbour, opened the door and walked straight in. Andrew Marks was standing behind a counter covered with papers and ledgers. He looked up as she entered, hoping it would be a customer. It wasn't and his face fell.

"Oh it's you!" he said

"It does a lady good to know she's appreciated Andrew!" Agnes replied tartly.

Andrew quickly realised it wasn't the best policy to upset the Old Towns oldest and wisest woman. It was said that Agnes could have a vicious tongue on her and, by the very nature of his wheeling's and dealings, the last thing Andrew needed was to make an enemy of someone like her. Anyway he liked Agnes. In his own way he saw her as the same sort of rogue he was, and they had shared some interesting times together.

"I'm sorry. It's a bit hectic this morning. I've got some cargoes held up. They're stuck somewhere between here and York. The roads are getting impassable you know!"

Agnes glanced towards the paperwork. "Legal or illegal?" She asked pointedly.

Andrew closed the ledger with more force than was necessary. "Legal, of course!"

Agnes placed the empty bottle on the counter in front of him. "I want one of these please." She said.

Andrew looked at the bottle as if he'd never seen such a thing before. "Agnes I don't know if you noticed but the sign outside says Ships Chandlery. I don't sell sherry."

"Andrew, I know what you do. You know I know. In fact we both know I know, so let's stop pretending. There's not a ships cat comes into this port without you knowing about it. You know exactly when and who brought the sherry in. You know where it comes from. You probably even know the name of the Spaniard who danced on the grapes."

Andrew capitulated. "A case came in day afore yesterday. Whitby John bought a bottle. The Commander of the Garrison bought another two, The Vicar up at St Mary's bought one and I think the landlord of the Beehive took some. There may be some left. Have a word with Ethan Newby, he's the Captain of a small Brig called "The Merchant", sails between Newcastle and Hull. He's the one that brought it in."

Andrew gave her directions as to where the ship was moored and, after a few pleasantries, Agnes pulled her shawl around her shoulders and set out into the cold once again. Despite the harbour being full of ships, from fishing boats to small traders, she found "The Merchant" easily. It was moored where Andrew said it would be, lying at anchor at the far end of the harbour among other merchant ships, sheltered under the headland and well away from the fishing boats that congregated nearer to the foreshore and the market. Agnes walked along the pier to where a thin narrow board connected the ship to the land. She was halfway down when her passage was halted by a large, thick set seaman. He stood with his arms crossed; his thick seaman's jersey and oilskin jacket made him seem bigger than he was. Just one glance at him and the word trouble screamed in Agnes's head.

"Sorry Missus. Can't go any further!"

Well at least he seemed polite, for now. "I want to see Captain Newby." She said in her best "little old lady lost" voice.

The man didn't move. "Aye that's as maybe but Captain Newby don't want to be seeing the likes of you!"

Agnes said nothing but stared up into the seaman's eyes. He blinked once and slowly moved to one side. He took her arm and very carefully led her onto the boat deck and to a small cabin at the rear of the deck. The door opened and the Captain emerged. He took one look at Agnes and turned to the sailor. He opened his mouth, but Agnes gave him one of her looks first.

She took the empty bottle out of her jacket. "Captain Newby I presume. Good day to you. I was told I could get one of these here!" she said.

The Captain stepped back, his attitude had changed completely. Normally Agnes tried to avoid using her magic to influence people, especially when it meant getting what she wanted. She believed in freedom of thought and actions. She also believed in consequences. The people around her lived their lives the best they could with as little interference from her as possible. It was that sometimes, just sometimes, people needed a little nudge in what she considered was the right direction. Right now the romantic needs of Whitby John took priority over a couple of merchant seamen. For one thing she owed Whitby John a bottle of sherry, and for another, it could, just, in the long run, mean that the drab interior of the Three Mariners might benefit from a female touch. Ripples and effects. It was all about ripples and effects.

Within minutes Agnes was back standing on the deck with a bottle shaped package in her hand. She thanked the captain profusely and he gave a small bow as the seaman, who she now figured was the first mate, carefully escorted her down the gangplank and onto the pier. She was halfway along the pier when she felt another tingle down her spine.

This time she knew it wasn't the cold. Something was warning her. Something was nagging at her, wanting her attention. She turned around and walked back towards "The Merchant". The pier was piled high with barrels and packing cases and all the things you normally expect to find on a busy dock side. She stepped over ropes, paused and stood behind a pile of barrels that had recently been unloaded from a nearby ship. She peered around them just in time to see Captain Newby return into the cabin. There was no sign of the sailor. At first there was nothing suspicious at all about the ship. It was moored up and looked just like every other ship on the quay side. However, the more she looked the more she felt that something wasn't right. She looked around, there was no one in sight. The air around her shimmered and she disappeared. A seagull hopped out from behind the barrels, waddled across the pier and launched itself in to the air above "The Merchant". It circled the ship a couple of times before dropping onto the roof of the cabin. The Captain was inside. At the bows the first mate suddenly emerged from the cargo hold. He made his way across the deck and entered the cabin. The seagull hopped further towards the window hoping to overhear their conversation.

The Captain looked up at the approach of the first mate. "Everything alright down there?"

The mate nodded. "Everything's stowed away safely."

The Captain nodded. "You can never be too careful in these tides, don't want that lot breaking free."

"I'll be glad when we've got rid of it. Gives me the willies having it down there."

The Captain turned and looked out towards the end of the pier and the open sea. "We won't have it much longer!"

The first mate stretched his back. "I wonder how that old woman knew were carrying sherry?"

The Captain shrugged. "She had an empty bottle, she probably knows someone who bought a case. You know what these small fishing towns are like, everybody knows everybody. Anyway it was you that let her onboard!"

As he spoke the mate pulled out a large knife, opened the clasp and began cleaning his fingernails with it. "I know. That's what's got me worried. One minute I was standing in front of her preventing her from coming aboard and the next I'm helping her up the gang plank."

The Captain chuckled. "You're going soft in your old age!"

The mate turned to face the captain. "What about you – you sold her that bottle without even asking questions."

The captain shrugged "She reminded me of my old Gran. I was always fond of my old Gran!"

He pulled the half sovereign out of his pocket and looked at it in his hand. "Well at least we made a profit out of it!"

"We could go ashore and have a drink." The mate said hopefully.

The captain shook his head. "Too risky. Suppose he comes back and finds the ship empty?"

The mate snarled. "He's only the servant. He can't tell us what to do."

"He's the servant of the bloke that pays our wages. We don't want him running back to his master telling tales of how we're unreliable now do we?"

The mate said something that Agnes couldn't quiet hear. She hopped nearer but the Captain stomped off into the cabin. The seagull hopped along the cabin roof and took off with two lazy beats of its wings. It circled the harbour a couple of times gaining height in the cool crisp air and flew off to merge with the rest of the flock on the Castle headland. A little while later the air shimmered at the side of a tumble down shed in a back yard. The figure of an elderly lady emerged from an alleyway and stepped onto Castlegate.

Back inside her kitchen Agnes sat down with a strong and very hot cup of Mr Tetley's finest tea. The temperature had dropped even further. She took the bottle of sherry out of her inside pocket and examined the bottle. That it was Spanish there was no doubt. That it had been smuggled into the harbour was also a certainty. What she couldn't work out was what it was doing on a merchant ship that traded between Hull and Newcastle. There again, all along the coast items and cargoes changed hands, trades and deals were being struck for merchandise that originated all over the world. It could have been picked up in Hull or Newcastle or any one of a dozen smaller ports between the two. Still at least Whitby John would be able to fulfil his promise to his lady.

The conversation the crew had held about the servant and master was a different puzzle. It seemed to Agnes that the ship and its crew were working for someone who didn't seem to sound like a normal shipping agent, if there was such a thing.

That night Agnes lay in her twenty first century bed unable to get to sleep. She turned on the bedside radio. The snow was still causing chaos. All the roads across the moors were blocked. As usual people were stranded in their cars. A helicopter had been called in to drop fodder for the sheep caught out up on the tops of the moors. She lay there pondering on the fact that no matter how far technology advanced, modern society is just as vulnerable to the weather as eighteenth century society was.

Eventually she drifted off only to be haunted by a nightmare. A vision of two red eyes came into her mind. In her dreams she was walking alongside the harbour and the eyes were watching from upstairs windows. Every time she spotted them they moved to a different building. They appeared in shop windows, from behind chimney stacks, in the gaps between houses. She began to run but the eyes kept up with her, appearing and disappearing. In her haste she tripped over a rope and fell headlong over the harbour wall. The sea was a long way down and as she fell, below her the eyes slowly drifted to the surface of the water coming up to meet her. She woke with a shudder just before she hit the surface.

She got up, dressed and walked downstairs into her kitchen. She pulled down a large ancient, silver platter that she filled with clear water. She placed in on her table, sat down and passed her hand over the water. It fizzed briefly and then cleared. She bent down and looked into the water. She could see an image of the harbour. There were a few yellow lights in windows of the buildings along the foreshore. Other lights bobbed and reflected off the pitch black sea. The moon appeared only to disappear behind a series of clouds blown in from the sea. The wind blew the smoke from the Old Town chimneys back over the town. Out of curiosity she looked for "The Merchant". It was still at its berth bobbing gently up and down on the incoming tide. A light shone in the cabin window and she could make out the shape of someone moving along the deck. It looked like the mate.

She moved onto the Castle and the headland. She heard a fox bark and an owl hoot. Up at the garrison she could see the Union Jack flying over the gatehouse. A light shone in the Commanders office. A guard sheltered by the side of the gate trying to keep out of the wind. Then something moved a shadow across the moon. It moved too fast for it to be a cloud. She scanned the scene once again but couldn't see anything. Whatever it was had been lost in the dark shadows of the buildings and chimneys. Perhaps it was a bird. She looked down at the Old Town and could see her own roof. She looked closer. There was a slight movement behind her chimney stack. She bent closer; suddenly the water was filled with the image of a pair of red ringed eyes. They were looking straight out of the water at her, echoing the images of her nightmare. Instinctively she pulled her head back and the eyes disappeared. She passed her hand over the platter and the water turned cloudy. She sat back heavily in her chair, the eyes still burning in her memory.

From nowhere Marmaduke suddenly appeared and rubbed his body around her legs. That gave her an idea. Before the cat realised what was happening he had been scooped up in her arms.

She walked down the cellar and walked through the door, remembering to let go of the cat as she did. When she appeared at the opposite side of the door, she was greeted by a tall, ginger man, bearded and wearing a black eye patch. He wore a battered leather jerkin and a pair of trousers, both of which had seen much better days. The ends of the trousers were tucked into the tops of a pair of beaten up riding boots. The handle of a knife poked out of the top of the right one. He stroked his moustache.

"What was all that about?" He asked

"I need to talk something through." Said Agnes

Marmaduke shrugged his shoulders. "Is that all? I thought there was some sort of emergency!"

"There might be!" Said Agnes as she turned around and walked back up the cellar steps.

They sat around the kitchen table drinking tea. Agnes was drinking out of her usual "Worlds Best Granny" mug whilst Marmaduke had poured his into a saucer and was busy lapping it up. Agnes watched frowning.

"You know that is really distracting."

Marmaduke raised an eyebrow "You want distraction? You try falling asleep as a cat on a cushion and waking up wearing a pair of boots!"

Agnes said nothing but pushed her chair back and stood up. She looked out of her kitchen window. A mist had fallen over the town and dawn was battling to force thin streaks of morning light through the damp greyness.

"I know what's needed!" She said and busied herself by rattling pots and pans and digging into the fridge. Soon, much to Marmaduke's delight, she had a full English breakfast on the go. Bacon, eggs, tomatoes, mushrooms, baked beans, fried bread. Marmaduke was actually drooling as the plate was put in front of him.

"Knife and fork please!" Agnes reminded him.

They ate in silence as outside day break arrived in a wash of damp grey and smoke smudged snow white, inside she cleaned her plate by wiping a piece of bread around it.

"Time for full stomach thinking!" she proclaimed.

Marmaduke stroked his whiskers and sat back as Agnes proceeded to tell him of the events of the last day, of the bottle of Spanish sherry, of the two sailors on board the "The Merchant", of the strange shadow that crossed the moon, of the eyes that first appeared in her dream and then re-appeared in her scrying bowl.

Marmaduke considered everything for a few minutes.

"So we have a boat with a mysterious cargo and its mate and captain. They're working for someone who communicates via a servant and do a bit of smuggling on the side. What's wrong with that? Just about every boat down there does a bit of smuggling from time to time."

"It smells wrong, I can't put my finger on it but it just doesn't feel right."

"Then you're dreaming about red eyes and they appear in your scrying bowl!" He stared across the table at her.

"Well?" she asked

Marmaduke averted his eyes.

She poured herself another cup of tea. "I'm not going mad you know. I'm not making it up. I have a feeling and my feelings are never wrong!"

Marmaduke nodded. He had lived with Agnes for many years and knew from great experience when to argue and when not to argue. This was one of those times when not to argue. Anyway she was right, when it came to feelings she was never wrong.

"Why don't you have a look on the roof?" he suggested.

Agnes shook her head. "I'd already thought of that. Not a lot of point, the snow hasn't started falling in 1779, yet. Not like the winter of 2014."

She nodded towards the window. Outside the grey air was now carrying small flakes of snow that danced and drifted passed the kitchen window. Marmaduke had a full stomach and began to feel drowsy. He was prevented from dropping asleep by a sharp poke in the ribs.

"Come on. Let's go for a walk along the harbourside. I've got to take Whitby John his bottle of sherry anyway!"

In1779 the morning was still bitter cold. An arctic chill was blowing in and a thick layer of frost lay on the cobbles and house roofs. Frost patterns covered the windows of the houses they passed. Inside fires were been lit and strands of smoke wafted from the chimneys.

Whitby John was at standing at the door of the Three Mariners when they arrived. He was looking anxiously up and down the road. His hands were thrust under his armpits in an attempt to keep them warm. His breath formed cold clouds that hung in front of his before dissolving into the crisp air. He spun round expectantly as Agnes and Marmaduke approached him.

"Oh it's you!" he said disappointedly.

"Always nice to be made welcome!" Agnes said tartly. "Especially when I'm bringing you a present!"

She held the bottle out and John took it. He turned it over in his hand and looked up at her.

"I won't ask how you managed to get a bottle!" he said. He gave a last look up and down the street and opened the door. "Come on, it's freezing out here. At least get a bit of warmth into both of you!"

They followed him into the bar where a large fire was just starting to take hold. Flames were roaring up the chimney. "It'll settle when the wind changes quarter." he said.

They sat in front of the fire. He pulled out a jug of ale and placed it by the fire. Then he sprinkled some herbs and spices into it and put an iron bar into the fire. He gave them a small tankard each.

"Mulled ale. That'll warm you up."

"What were you looking for out there?" Agnes asked as the hot poker emerged from the fire glowing bright orange. The landlord plunged it into the jug of liquid. It bubbled and fizzed and a cloud of scented steam filled the bar. He poured out a measure into each tankard.

"Not a what, a who! One of our Edith's cousins has a place up on the moors. He was meant to deliver a cart-load of peat yesterday morning. Haven't seen hide nor hair of him."

"Probably the bad weather held him up."

The landlord looked out of the window. "It's not as

bad as its going to be. Any way he lives up there, he's used to worse than this. A bit of frost and the cold shouldn't prove a problem."

"Perhaps his horse has gone lame or something's happened to his cart!" Offered Marmaduke.

The landlord leant forward towards Agnes and lowered his voice. "Look Agnes, I know about you and your reputation, I know you can do… you know, things! Can't you have a look; you know use a crystal ball or something!"

Agnes looked straight back at him. "You mean use a bit of magic?"

The landlord grimaced at the word magic. "Agnes, we all know you're more than a healer."

Agnes looked across at Marmaduke. He gave a slight nod of his head.

"Fetch me a platter filled with water and put it on that table." She asked.

The landlord went off to find a suitable platter.

"Do you think it's a good idea?"

Agnes looked up at Marmaduke and took a deep drink of the mulled ale. "I think it's worth it. He's trying not to show it but I think he's genuinely very worried about the missing cart and its driver."

The landlord reappeared carefully carrying a large platter. Water splashed over its side as he tried to manoeuvre it to the table without too much spillage. He placed it in the middle of the table and looked up at Agnes.

"That do for you?" He asked. Agnes nodded and walked up to the table. John pulled a rickety chair out for her. She looked at it, gave it a shake and, satisfied it would hold her, sat down.

She nodded towards the landlord who was settling himself down at the opposite side of the table. "You better sit here, next to me. You can recognise your relation if we see him."

Whitby John nervously picked up his chair, placed it next to Agnes and sat down. He hadn't encountered magic before and wasn't sure he was going to like the experience.

"Where are you going to look?" he asked

Agnes turned her head to look at him. "It all depends on what route you think he'll have taken down from the moors."

The landlord scratched his head for a minute in deep thought. Eventually he had a route worked out in his mind.

"He'd come down from Allerston Moor…. through Langdale, then cut across through Hackness and onto Scalby…"

Agnes bent over the platter of water and made a move with her hand; the water fizzed slightly and turned cloudy.

"… then drop down through Falsgrave."

"Let's start from the beginning." she suggested. "Let's find Allerston Moor."

She peered into the water as it cleared to reveal a wintry, moorland scene. The deep frost had turned most of the landscape white. There were slight snow flurries across her vision. The weather was deteriorating up there. She passed over the landscape of trees and small valleys, occasionally passing small pockets of habitation where nothing moved. She moved her hand and the scene changed. Once again she looked down on a patch of deserted moorland dotted with occasional stony outcrops and desolate trees.

Eventually she discovered a drovers road. There was movement. A small figure well wrapped up and bend double against the cold and the wind was leading a team of six squat sturdy horses across the open moor. They were loaded down with large bundles that lurched precariously from side to side as the horses took their dogged steps. She looked up at Whitby John. He shook his head.

She moved forward along the road until it passed through a wooded area in the middle of a wide valley. It was deserted. She followed it out of the valley and back onto the bleakness of the top of the moor. She came to a crossing point where a second drover's road leading north joined the main track. The place was marked by a large, ancient stone cross. She had almost dismissed the area and was about to pass on when a slight movement off the road caught her eye. Some yards beyond the cross, parallel with the northern path was a slight depression in the moor where a stream ran into a large pond. At the side of the pond, almost sinking out of sight was an overturned cart. Its contents were spilt across the moor. It was a load of cut peat turfs. She looked up towards Whitby John. His face was white, with a trembling finger he was pointing to an area at the side of the image. Agnes moved the view until the area was in the centre of the platter. She bent down to look closer. Now she could see the image of a body. It was difficult to see at first as it seemed to be half in and half out of the water among some tall reeds and grasses. The frost had covered it, the cold whiteness merging it with the rest of the moorland. On looking closer it was obvious that it had been badly mauled. Small pieces of ripped clothing were scattered around. One of them flapped in the wind, causing the movement that had caught Agnes's eye. She grimaced when she saw what little remained of the face. The body had been so badly mutilated that few recognisable features could be made out. She passed her hand over the platter and the water turned misty. She gave a sigh and sat back in her chair. She said nothing. There was nothing to say.

Marmaduke walked across to the bar and took two glasses from the rickety shelf. He took a bottle of French Brandy from under the bar and poured two large measures. He walked back to the table and placed them in front of Agnes and Whitby John. John drank his off in one gulp. Agnes looked at the full glass and shook her head slightly. John noticed, took her glass and downed that one as well.

He looked up at Agnes. "We have to get his body off the moor!"

"Won't someone up there go looking for him?" Marmaduke asked

"Who?" Answered Whitby John, "There's only us as knows he's missing, and that's cos he didn't arrive here. Them at home won't begin to miss him till he's due back, and that's another two days."

"By that time there won't be much for anyone to find!" Marmaduke added.

Shakily the landlord stood up and moved towards the door that led to his private rooms. "There's things I need to do, arrangements I need to make."

They listened as they heard his footsteps going quickly up the wooden stairs. They waited till they heard the sound of a door shutting. Only then Agnes nodded at Marmaduke

"Something attacked him and caused those wounds. We need to have a look at him as soon as possible, before anything else gets to him, poor soul!"

"What else?"

Agnes looked across towards the fire. "There's buzzards and other birds of prey for a start, then there's crows and foxes, there's plenty of creatures up on the moors that live off carrion!"

Marmaduke shook his head. "You know what I mean. There's no creature living up there that can drag a man off his horse, rip his throat out and shred his face!"

"Another man could!"

A sound from upstairs caused Marmaduke to turn towards the door and he lowered his voice. "You know what I mean. He hasn't remembered yet but no doubt everyone in the bar will. That body is near to the place where them dead sheep where found."

"I had noticed. What's even worse is that they'll also remember Old Sam's story of the Barghest!" Agnes said as she picked up the platter and walked across to the bar.

Marmaduke watched as she opened the door, poured the water into the street, gave it a wipe and carefully replaced it on a shelf. "Don't tell me you believe in the old legend?" he asked.

Agnes looked up at him and narrowed her eyes. "Just let's say I don't disbelieve it!"

"Are you going to let him go up there by himself?"

"Of course not, we're both going!"

"It'll take a couple of days at the least."

Agnes smiled. "Not the way we're going. It's only mid morning now. We'll be there before evening. You get off home. Get some warm clothes ready. I'll be along shortly!"

Marmaduke said nothing but turned and left the bar. As he walked into the street he noticed the water from the platter had already frozen into a puddle of ice. Agnes heard footsteps and went to the bottom of the stairs just as Whitby John emerged. He was already dressed for the journey. He was wearing a large, oiled, fisherman's pullover, a badly hand knitted scarf and a huge riding coat that almost touched the floor as he walked. Underneath Agnes could see he was wearing a pair of old battered riding boots.

"I'm closing up and getting off. I'll hire a horse from Bradshaw's Livery stables. With a bit of luck I'll be up there afore nightfall."

Agnes patted his hand. "You get off. I'll see to things here. Hopefully it'll work itself out. Things have a habit of working themselves out!"

John left the bar leaving the door open behind him. Agnes went across to the fire and built it up. She opened the remaining shutters and flooded sunlight into the room. She marched to the back door opened it and pulled out an ear. Attached to the ear was the head of Baccy Lad.

"I don't know how long you've been listening behind the door but you know what they say about people who listen to other peoples conversations!"

Baccy Lad frantically shook his head. "I only just come. John wanted a bottle of sherry and I knew where to get my hands on one. Here it is." He produced a bottle from behind his back and offered to Agnes. She took it and examined it closely.

"This isn't the same sherry."

Baccy Lad shook his head. "I know but sherry's sherry, anyway I knew where to lay my hands on a spare bottle. Better than nothing."

Agnes looked at the bottle again. "This wouldn't by any chance, be a bottle from a shipment that was delivered to the Queens Arms the other day?"

Baccy Lad shook his head.

Agnes sighed. "I know where this bottle came from and you know where you got it from. The only person who doesn't know where it is, is its rightful owner. Now instead of me being a dutiful citizen and telling him I could choose to keep quiet. On one condition."

Baccy Lad knew when to concede a point. Like everyone else in the Old Town, he knew Agnes as a wise woman, which was a polite way of saying she was a witch. He'd never actually seen her turn anyone into a frog or a newt but there had been some very strange rumours about her and he didn't want to be the one who found out the hard way.

"What condition?" he asked

"That you look after this bar for an hour or so. John's had to rush off to see to some unexpected family business. Someone will be down to take charge soon enough."

Baccy Lad could hardly believe his luck. His head bobbed up and down so quickly Agnes thought he might do himself some harm. She pointed towards the bar.

"Well you'd better get started. Stand behind the bar and whilst there's no one here use this!" She threw a cleaning cloth at him and Agnes walked towards the doorway. Just before leaving the bar she turned around.

"Mind you, if anything does go missing you'll find yourself croaking up by the Castle pond!"

Baccy Lad froze to the spot and watched the door close behind her. She wouldn't, surly she couldn't. But deep down he had a very nasty feeling that she could, and would.

Before she went home Agnes had one more thing to do. She slipped into a deserted yard, the air shimmered and all that remained were specks of dust floating in a pool of morning sunlight.

Mrs Pateley, a widow of this parish, was sitting in her drawing room. She was concentrating on her needlework. She wasn't very good at it but her friends told her she needed to keep busy. That busy hands kept grief away. She had lost her husband over a year ago. He had been swept off the deck of his own whaler somewhere off the coast of Greenland. He'd been dead three months before the news reached her. A knock on her door caused her to jump and prick her finger. She sat and listened. There was a second knock. As she rose to her feet she wondered why her maidservant hadn't answered it. She shouted her name but there was no sign of the girl, an eerie silence hung around the house. If she had looked through her window she would have seen a strange sight. Outside nothing was moving. The trees bent with the wind, but they were not moving. A flock of seagulls hung suspended in the air. Across the road Mrs Storr was on her way from the church to visit her daughter lower down the road. She was frozen with one foot caught stepping in front of the other, as if she was a statue. Annoyed Mrs Pateley opened the door herself. There was an old woman standing there. Mrs Pateley recognised her as the old wise woman that some people she knew went to for certain ointments and lotions. Mrs Pateley didn't really agree with that sort of thing and relied on the medical knowledge of her Doctor who lived in a big house up on Ramshill, a much better address. She tried to remember the old woman's name.

"The names Agnes, we need to talk!" The woman held out her hand and sailed right passed and into the hallway. Mrs Pateley turned round. She was just about to deliver a complaint about forwardness when she noticed the woman's eyes. They stared at her, then the pupils seemed to expand, getting bigger and bigger. It seemed as if she were falling into them.

Fifteen minutes later she was seated back in her drawing room, the needlework forgotten as she realised she had admitted to the old woman her own, very private feelings about the widower who ran the Three Mariners. She was both shocked and surprised to discover that the old woman knew her history. That she had been born in service and had spent sometime behind a bar in a public house in Rotherhithe before meeting the sea captain she would be married to for the next twenty years of her life. That was why she had been the perfect choice when it came to finding someone to manage the inn whilst John had to attend to some urgent family business. It all made perfect sense, somehow.

As she sat in front of her discarded sewing Mrs Pateley was surprised to realise that she actually felt happy, and that she hadn't experienced that feeling for a lot of years. She smiled to herself as she hurried off to make the necessary arrangements. Outside in the street Mrs Storr paused. She thought she heard a door shut, but there was no one in the street. She continued walking to her daughter's house as the trees bent in the wind and the seagulls whirled overhead.

Chapter Three

When Agnes arrived back home Marmaduke was ready and waiting. He was wearing a heavy coat under which she could see a sword. She could also see the shape of a pistol tucked into the inside of his jerkin, another was tucked into his belt. A knife poked out from the top of his boot, and she had no doubt others were hidden among the folds of his clothing. He looked ready to fight a one man war.

She went into the kitchen and selected a number of small bottles and pots which she carefully put into her carpet bag. She turned to Marmaduke.

"Ready?"

He nodded and they walked out of the front door. At the end of the street they turned right up Castlegate Hill. As they walked up the frosty cobbles Agnes made a series of small signs with her fingers. Marmaduke became aware that the scenery was slipping past him as a blur. Within a matter of minutes they were on the edge of town. Another couple of minutes they were approaching the village of Cloughton where Agnes turned onto a roadway that led up towards the moors. Ahead of them they could make out a lone figure on horseback. They soon caught him up and Agnes moved her fingers to weave an additional spell that included the horse and rider. It took another fifteen minutes for them to arrive on top of the moor where the ancient cross stood starkly pointing up to the sky like an accusing finger. Around them the pale sunlight was melting the frost and softening the frozen ground. Whitby John looked around him in surprise. He was about to say something but Marmaduke just shook his head.

"Better not to ask!" he said quietly.

John climbed off his horse and tethered it to the

base of the stone cross. Marmaduke slithered down a slope and walked towards the pool. The body was where they first saw it, half in and half out of the water. A thin layer of ice covered the pool and had formed over the body, but the weak morning sun had melted it, revealing the extent of the injuries of John's unfortunate relation. John turned his head and made the sign of the cross. Agnes found an old piece of cloth and covered the head.

Marmaduke squatted on his haunches and examined the body. He lifted the cloth and looked at the huge head wounds. He looked long and hard before covering it up again and began to examine the frozen earth. He worked slowly and methodically moving away from the body inch by inch.

A few feet away from the body he found a large paw print impressed in the hard mud. It was so deep it held a small puddle of water over which ice had formed. He crouched on all fours and began to sniff the ground as he moved along. Eventually he found more of the paw prints. They led across the moor heading towards a small wooded valley.

As Marmaduke did the tracking, between them Agnes and John lifted the body onto Johns hired horse and strapped it down so it was hanging across the saddle. They went back and looked at the cart. It was missing a wheel which they found half-stuck in the mud at the far side of the pond. Agnes looked under the cart and saw that its axle was shattered. She shook her head at John.

"I doubt that even the use of magic can do much for the cart." She said. They stood by its side and watched as Marmaduke scampered this way and that over the moorland, sniffing at the long grass and moving large ferns with his hands. As he watched Whitby John couldn't help but notice how cat like Marmaduke's movements were.

Eventually Marmaduke returned to the upturned cart. He jumped up on its overturned side and sat down and explained what he had discovered.

"I think I know what happened. Judging by the signs and tracks I would say that the attacker followed the cart and its driver over the moor. The driver knew he was being followed and tried to get the most speed out of his horse. You can see back there how the hoof prints increase the stride pattern. I'm not sure if they managed a gallop, but they did go fast, fast enough that when the wheel hit a stone the cart jumped into the air and turned over. I'm pretty certain the driver was thrown onto the road and hit his head on a rock. There's a large one by the side of the road just over there, not that far from where we found the body. It has a mass of matted hair and blood on it. I've also found drag marks. The horse broke free, you can see where the reins snapped, and headed off down the valley. The creature didn't bother following it though; it turned round and attacked the unconscious driver. From the paw prints I would say the attacker was a dog, a very large dog.

Whitby John crossed himself. "Did he suffer?"

As he looked up at Agnes she noticed how white and drawn his face had become.

Marmaduke shook his head. "I'm pretty certain he was either dead or unconscious when the creature attacked him. Judging by the amount of blood and hair on the rock I would say he took a hell of a blow to the head back there."

Agnes wrapped her arms around her own body a couple of times and looked up at the sky. She gave a small shiver. "Come on, there's nothing more we can do up here, lets get him home to Allerston before the snow comes."

Black clouds were beginning to form on the horizon. They left the cart where it was and the small, sad party walked across the moor leading Johns horse that carried the body back home along the drover's road.

Allerston wasn't a village, it was barely a hamlet. It was a small farm and two smaller cottages huddled in the slight depression on the moor. It was sheltered from the weather by a bank of trees that formed a small wood that stretched under the crest of a hill. As they approached a woman peered out of the building Agnes assumed was the farmhouse.

"It's Joan, his wife." John said.

Agnes stopped the horse and nodded towards John. "Would you like a few moments to explain?"

John stopped "What do I say to her?"

Marmaduke gave a shrug. "That he had an accident, fell off the cart and hit his head."

John looked around towards the farm house "And what about the wounds?"

Agnes sighed. "Just tell her the truth, that his body was ravaged by carrion crows, or buzzards."

"I don't mention the large dog?"

Agnes shook her head. "No, don't mention the large dog, at least not until we know something more definite."

John left them and walked up to the woman. She recognised him and instinctively she could tell something was wrong. He placed his arm around her and spoke to her in a low voice. Agnes and Marmaduke weren't sure what he said but she suddenly let go of a huge kerning scream and then dissolved into a series of deep racking sobs. Without looking behind him John led her back into the farmhouse.

Roused by the noise a face appeared at the window of the nearest cottage. Marmaduke looked around. "Who else lives here?"

Agnes looked at the face. "I've no idea. Let's find out."

She walked across to the cottage door and knocked. It was opened by a pale faced young woman. Behind her a number of small dirty faced children peered out from behind a wooden door. As she stood there Agnes became aware of a loose flock of feral hens that pecked at her feet in the vain hope of finding something to eat. The woman looked across to the horse that was still carrying its grim bundle. She then glanced across to the farm house.

"Did the dog get him?" She asked. A hint of terror was in her voice.

Agnes patted the woman's shoulder. "And what dog would that be?" She asked gently.

The woman pulled her shabby shawl tighter across her shoulders. Agnes took a step forward.

"Why don't I come in, where we can talk more easily!"

Without question the woman stepped to one side and allowed Agnes to enter the small building. As she lowered her head to get through the door she turned to Marmaduke.

"Can you try to find somewhere to lay him out?"

Marmaduke simply nodded and turned to walk back to the horse.

The inside of the cottage was small and dark, but thanks to an open hearth and a peat fire, it was warm, bordering on cosy. The room held a dresser that displayed some plates, a jug and a bowl. A spoon lay discarded on the floor. In the middle of the room was a table with two chairs. On one of the chairs was a pile of dirty clothing. Through a doorway that Agnes assumed led to a small kitchen, a thin mist of steam was rising.

"My name's Emma by the way, my husbands the shepherd. I've just started the washing!" The woman said hoping to explain the pile of clothing and the steam.

Agnes smiled. "I won't keep you long!"

She looked at the doorway where the four little faces still watched. Agnes rose and walked towards them. Their eyes widened but they held their place. Agnes fiddled in her bag. Suddenly one at a time she produced four bright shiny red apples. She bent down and gave one to each child. They looked towards their mother. She smiled and nodded.

"Say thank you to the lady!"

The four children all said "Thank you!" as politely as possible. The two smaller ones even attempted a slight curtsey. Agnes held back a chuckle and instead gave them a bright smile. "Now why don't you all go upstairs and let me and your mother have a little chat?"

Again they all looked towards their mother. She smiled at them. "Up to you room, you can come back down when the kind lady has gone!"

The four children turned and scampered up the small staircase and disappeared out of sight.

"Thank you!" the woman said as she moved the armful of washing onto the table itself.

Agnes took the offered seat and beckoned for the woman to sit as well. She shook her head. "I'll put the kettle on first." She said as she slipped into the kitchen.

As she left Agnes turned and looked out of the small window. Marmaduke had led the horse to the far side of the farm to a low building that looked as if it could be a barn and was cutting the body free from its harness. She turned as the woman entered the room carrying two chipped mugs steaming with tea. She placed them on the table and sat down herself.

Agnes blew on the hot tea. "Is your husband near?"

The woman shook her head. "He's up on the far moor bringing in the sheep."

"Now Emma, have you lost any sheep recently?"

The woman clasped her hands together and nodded nervously.

"When was this?"

"We lost one last week. Peter found it over towards

Fylingdales Moor."

Agnes raised an eyebrow and, after a brief pause the woman continued. "We lost another two, this week. The day before yesterday. Peter found the bodies just down the valley."

She pointed at the far wall beyond which, Agnes assumed, lay the valley in question.

"When did your husband leave?" Agnes asked noting her nervousness.

The woman glanced out of the window. "Before dawn this morning. He needed an early start to get there and back before nightfall. He says they will be safer here, off the moor."

A penny suddenly dropped at the back of Agnes' mind. "You thought it was your husband we'd found!"

The woman let go a deep sob. Tears began flowing down her face. Agnes patted her on the shoulder. "Let's make sure he's safe shall we?"

The woman looked up, her eyes asked the question but her mouth remains closed.

Agnes rose and walked into the kitchen. It was full of steam, a large wash tub sat at the side of the room with a log fire burning underneath it. The door to a small yard was open. Outside she could see the hills and the moors. By the door was a large heavy wooden bucket. Obviously there was a pump or a well close by. She took a small platter she found and filled it from the kettle. She carried back into the other room and placed it on the table. She then sat over it and moved her hand. The water fizzed and went cloudy, then went clear once again. She leant forward and peered into the platter. To start she scanned the nearby moorland in a wide sweep. She didn't have to wait long. She picked up a line of sheep all walking in a line. Two sheep dogs were herding them across the moor and a shepherd was walking just behind them. Agnes noticed he was carrying a large wooden staff, and kept looking anxiously behind him. Agnes estimated he was about a mile away from the farmstead. As she watched she noticed another movement on the moor. At first it seemed to be a large black shadow that appeared and disappeared in the dips and hollows of the open moor. However in her mind there was no doubt what it was, it was what she had feared. Very quietly and in a steady voice Agnes glanced up at the anxious woman.

"Could you go and fetch my companion. Tell him it is urgent!" she said.

The woman said nothing but rose wide eyed and left the cottage. As soon as she was outside she broke into a run. Agnes looked back down at the vision in the platter. She could make out the line of sheep. They were uneasy and skittish; the two working dogs were finding it hard to keep them under control. She saw the black shape. It was moving across the moor like a bad shadow. Agnes had no doubts that it was stalking the flock and its shepherd. Suddenly the door burst opened and Marmaduke rushed in. She said nothing but pointed at the bowl of water. Marmaduke looked over her shoulder. She pointed at the moving shadow.

"He needs assistance."

Marmaduke understood the gravity of the situation straight away.

"How far away are they?"

"About a mile."

"I'll be there in ten minutes, fifteen at the most!" He walked out of the cottage and began to run across the farmyard. As he reached the other side the air around him shimmered. The figure of a man dissolved and the figure of a large cat could be seen bounding up the hill onto the moors.

Agnes bent over the water in the platter searching for the black shadow. She scanned around the flock of sheep that were now being herded along at a fast trot. The dogs were running more urgently, Agnes could see they sensed danger. She picked up a movement at the top of her vision. She shifted the viewpoint and saw that the shadow was running along a narrow depression that ran parallel to the trackway the sheep were following. She realised it was trying to position itself between the flock and the farmstead and cut the flock off. She had to move quickly. She concentrated her mind and narrowed her eyes. Out on the moor the sky had cleared, it was a bright but cold morning. From nowhere a bolt of lightning cracked like a whip. Its force crashed at the head of the narrow depression. A sudden fire flared up blocking the passage of the black shadow. Knowing its route was blocked the shadow turned and scrambled out of the gully and onto the open moor. For the first time she could now actually see it clearly. It was as she'd feared, a huge black dog, about the size of a small pony. As it stood and sniffed the air she could see the outline of its large head. Its nostrils flared and it drew its lips back revealing a blood red maw lined with sharp fangs. Drool dribbled and flecked from its jaw. It was looking at the line of sheep. She concentrated her thoughts once again and another fireball of lightening hit the moor between the sheep and the creature. The creature flinched and lowered itself onto its stomach. It growled. Across the moor the sheep were now running, a panic had spread through the flock. The dogs ran alongside, barking and snarling keeping the sheep in a straight line. Behind them the shepherd jogged along. He was doing his best to keep up but Agnes could see he was losing ground. The dog could see it as well. It began to half-walk, half-crawl towards him. Agnes let go another ball of lightening. It screeched through the air and hit the moor again between the shepherd and the dog. The dog reared up on its hind legs and a long ear piercing howl burst out of its throat. It was enough to panic the sheep and they began to stampede. Fortune had it that they continued in the same direction of the drive. The two dogs continued at their task, now they were running at full belt, snapping, growling and barking, keeping the flock pointed forward. The shepherd was left behind. He looked exhausted, he staggered, tripped and fell to his knees. The black dog was watching and sensed its opportunity. It began to pad slowly towards the man who was now frozen with fear. It tongue lolled from side to side. Agnes watched as the scene began to unfold in front of her. She moved her hand and was about to release another bolt of lightning when she saw a shimmer in the air between the dog and the shepherd. As she watched the space was filled by the figure of a large, broad shouldered, ginger haired man with an eye patch.

The sudden apparition caused the dog to stop. It stood examining the figure, panting and drooling, it seemed confused. It sniffed the air and lolled its head from side to side. Then it made its decision. It leapt.

Marmaduke stood his ground. His hands flashed to his sides and he pulled out the two pistols. As the dog was in mid air Marmaduke side stepped and fired each pistol one after the other. One bullet missed clipping the dog's ear. The second buried itself buried itself in the creatures shoulder. The dog yelped and twisted in the air. As it moved through the air its jaws snapped at Marmaduke, missing by a matter of inches. He dropped the pistols and drew his sword. There was no need. The dog hit the ground, rolled and gained its feet. It stood and glowered at Marmaduke, a trickle of blood dripping down its shoulders. It let out a long mournful howl, turned and loped off across the moor. Within strides it had dropped into a depression in the ground and disappeared from view.

Marmaduke waited until it he was sure the creature was not returning and then bent down and picked up his pistols. He walked across to the shepherd who had now dragged himself across to a large rock and was crouching behind it wide eyed with terror. Marmaduke offered his hand and the man gripped his arm. Marmaduke pulled him to his feet.

"Can you walk?" he asked.

"Try stopping me!" The shepherd replied.

Together they set off down the track after the sheep, in the direction of the farmstead.

Agnes passed her hand over the platter, the water clouded over. She pushed her chair away from the table and stood up. She looked across to the shepherd's wife. She was standing frozen to the spot, still staring at the platter of water. Agnes placed her hand on the woman's shoulder and very gently moved her fingers. The woman blinked and looked around her as if waking from a dream. There was the sound of a door closing and Agnes looked out of the doorway. Whitby John had left the farmhouse and was walking across the yard. Agnes went out to meet him when a noise caused her to turn around. Coming down the track leading off the moor were a hundred or so sheep at full gallop. Agnes turned towards John. He stood rooted to the spot looking with amazement at the sea of white wool charging towards him. Agnes spun around and made a swift gesture with her right hand. The air around John shimmered and a slight blue aura appeared around him. The leading sheep suddenly veered to one side and the flock followed, some to his right some to his left. From where Agnes stood he appeared like a tall lighthouse as the sea of sheep swept passed him, standing with his mouth wide open in amazement, his arms folded across his chest, bracing himself for an impact that never came. The leading sheep arrived at the far end of the farmyard and found their progress blocked by a sturdy fence. They stopped, some turned around, within seconds they became a huge writhing mass of bleating wool. Suddenly the two dogs were among them, snapping, growling, twisting and turning, gaining control. Soon the sheep were quiet. Agnes made another movement with her hand. John stepped forward and wiped the seat from his forehead with the sleeve of his coat.

"Now that's a sight you don't often see!" he commented.

Agnes looked up at his face. It held no trace of humour. She wondered to herself whether he was being ironic. It annoyed her that she couldn't tell.

The noise in the yard brought out the farmers widow. Her face was set in a grim mask. Her eyes were red. There were still marks down her cheeks where tears had run down her face. Agnes looked across to John. He replied with a brief nod. The woman looked across to the sheep.

"The shepherd is safe. We're just bringing him down off the moor now!" Agnes said.

The woman turned and looked at her

"The Dog?" she asked.

Agnes could see no point in sugaring the pill. The woman lived up here on the moor. She knew the legends; she was no stranger to hardship.

She nodded once. "I believe it was, as you say, The Dog!" she said.

The farmer's widow wiped her face with the back of her sleeve and grimly nodded towards the sheep. "It'll be back for them."

"Maybe, maybe not." As Agnes spoke another part of her mind was working out the details of a shielding spell. She measured and reckoned. She knew she could cast a spell to protect the sheep, she wasn't sure whether she could include the farmhouse, the cottage and the outbuildings.

John led the three women back into to farmhouse and into the kitchen. As she entered Agnes looked around. It was a spacious, well used and functional room with a large table at its centre A Welsh dresser took up most of one wall, its shelves displaying a selection of pewter plates and copper pots and pans. A fire blazed in the hearth where a blackened iron kettle hung on a spigot, suspended over the flames. Bunches of dried herbs hung from the low beams. Hams and other cured meats hung further away from the fire. Agnes approved. It was the type of kitchen she would have if she lived up on the moor.

Despite her grief Joan insisted on brewing and pouring a pot of tea. As they sipped the hot liquid Agnes began to notice small details, the tell tale signs of the man who once lived here and whose body was now lying in the outhouse. A well used clay pipe lay on the mantelshelf. A long weather coat hung behind the door, a pair of old boots were tucked away in the corner. Each of them a poignant reminder of the life that had been taken.

They drank their tea in silence when they heard the sound of footsteps. John opened the door to reveal Marmaduke striding across the yard half dragging half carrying the shepherd. Then Emma ran forward pushing John to one side in her haste to get to and hold her man. She was beaten by the two sheep dogs that ran up to him barking and yapping, eager to jump up and try to lick his face. The shepherd smiled as he bent down and greeted each one in turn. Then he said something and moved his hands and the dogs returned to guard the sheep. The wife took her husband by the arm and carefully walked him across the yard to their own cottage. John beckoned for Marmaduke to enter into the farmhouse kitchen. Agnes remained in the yard. She knew she had to do something to protect these people. She looked across to the flock of sheep. They had settled, the two dogs lay on their stomachs their heads resting on their two front paws making sure the flock stayed where they were. She stood in the middle of the yard and raised her arms towards the sky. One of the dogs raised its head to watch her as she moved her fingers, tracing out an invisible pattern in the sky. Very briefly a bright web of light spun out from her fingers and rose higher and higher in the air slowly spinning and turning, spreading further and further from her. When it reached the edges of the surrounding hills she dropped her arms and the cobweb dropped over the valley enclosing the farm house, the cottage, the yard, the outbuildings and the sheep. She sent her mind out to its edges to check for any gaps before she was sure that nothing would break through her protective spell. Satisfied she turned and re-entered the farmhouse and joined the others around the table.

As she entered the room Agnes nodded towards Joan and John sat around the kitchen table. Marmaduke stood in the background. His hands were clasped around a cup. He sniffed the steam and warmed his hands as he sipped the hot liquid.

Agnes was about to speak but was interrupted by the door opening and the shepherd and his wife entered into the room.

"We thought we'd better come across and see what we can do to help." said Peter said.

Joan nodded and they both sat on a settle under the widow that looked out onto the yard. As they settled themselves down Agnes looked up.

"We can't stay for long though. I've got the little ones to think about." As she spoke Emma looked across the yard towards her own cottage.

"Where are they?" asked Agnes

Emma turned to Agnes. "I put them to doing the

washing – I half expect the kitchen to be ankle deep in water when we get back!"

Agnes looked up. "Better get straight to business then. I have put some protection around the entire hamlet, including the sheep." She added looking at the shepherd.

Joan sniffed and wiped her face with the back of her sleeve. "John says you're a witch!" She said

Agnes smiled. "Yes I am – does anyone have a problem with that?"

No one said a word.

Whitby John gave a small forced cough. "I didn't actually say..."

Agnes cut him off. "No, I never thought you said anything."

The shepherd's wife looked up at Agnes. "I think it might have been your trick with the platter of water...."

Agnes smiled "Yes, I suppose that was a bit of a give away!"

Emma suddenly stood up and walked towards the window. As she spoke she looked out across the moors at the grey clouds covering the valley.

"If you go down the valley you'll be told we're all good God fearing folk around here, and for the most part we are, but our parents and grandparents, aye and them afore that, came from these moors and they learnt us the legends and told us of the old ways. If you came across our preacher he'd say that what you stand for is against the teachings of the church. What we say is that the legends and stories are older than our church. Some of them are etched in the stones of the moor themselves."

Agnes raised her eyebrows; she hadn't been prepared for such a speech, especially from the young woman.

She looked up at the shepherd. He simply shook his head. "I don't care what you are, all I know is that you helped to get me off that moor."

Joan suddenly spoke. As the words came out of her mouth her voice cracked with held in emotion. "I have to bury my husband!"

John put his arm around her "Now Emma, don't fret. I'll see to things."

Marmaduke stepped forward. "I'll go down to the church. See if I can find the priest and make the arrangements!"

Agnes shook her head. "No. I'll do that. I think you'd better stay here, at least for tonight. Just to make sure my spell holds. The same with you John."

John brushed an invisible mark from the front of his jacket. "Aye they'll have to drink at the Beehive for the next few days. I hate to give him the business but family comes first."

Agnes smothered a smile. "I wouldn't worry about the Mariners if I were you. I'm sure you'll find it'll be business as normal when you get back."

John wasn't convinced. "Happen...."

Agnes stood up. "I'm going to go down the valley. I need to follow some tracks, and I'll visit the priest on your behalf on my way down. Then I'll pop round to the Mariners. I need to pick something up from home."

She looked out of the window, "I'll be back by the morning at the latest!"

Both John and the shepherd stood up. "Nay lass. You can't...."

Agnes raised her hand palm upwards towards them. "I can, and I will. All I ask is that you stay here inside the Farmyard. The protection won't work if any of you venture beyond that far wall. Like I said I'll be back as soon as possible."

She stood up. "Marmaduke, a word if you please!"

Marmaduke walked her to the door and opened it allowing her to step out into the farm yard

She turned and as she spoke the cold air linked with her breath forming clouds of steam between her words. "I'm going to follow the tracks. See where they lead to."

Marmaduke nodded and wrinkled his nose. "I could smell them. They were rank! I could save you a lot of time and trouble."

Agnes shook her head. "No I need you to keep an eye on them in there. Anyway I said I wanted to follow them, not hunt them down."

Marmaduke raised an eyebrow "There's a difference?"

Agnes almost smiled. "There is with you. I want to observe and see what we're facing rather than go in all guns blazing! Speaking of which."She nodded at the pistols tucked into his belt. "If you hear anything untoward, shoot first and ask questions later."

Now Marmaduke smiled "If I shoot first there won't be anything left to ask questions of."

Agnes simply stroked her chin "That might be a good thing. Just look after them."

Marmaduke nodded and Agnes turned and walked across the yard towards the track they arrived on, but as she approached the wall the air around her shimmered and she simply faded from view.

Seconds later a large black crow rose up into the air, caught a breeze and spiralled up into the sky. Marmaduke watched until the tiny dot disappeared into the grey clouds. He turned around and went back into the farmhouse kitchen.

Chapter Four

As she soared up into the air Agnes became the crow. She allowed the crows nature to find the air currents that allowed her to drift effortlessly over the wintery landscape laid out below her. She concentrated her non crow brain and soon she began to see the tracks laid out below her. They appeared like small neon like glowing dots that as she glided closer to the earth she could make out as large paw prints. She knew she was on the right track. After a couple of miles the prints suddenly veered to the right and entered into a large wooded area. She circled the wood but could not make out any trace of the tracks leaving it. She allowed the crow to settle on the top of one of the taller trees and took her bearings. She realised that she was near to the road that led across the moors linking the two towns of Scarborough and Whitby. The road was pitted with the tracks and wheel ruts of the carters and drovers that moved goods up and down the coast. One set of tracks looked fresher than the rest. The hard rimmed wheels of the cart had broken the ice that formed over the puddles and semi frozen mud. The tracks led towards Scarborough.

She took to the air once again and allowed the air currents to lift her higher and higher until she could see the road as it dropped and twined its way across the moor. She was almost on the outskirts of the town before she spotted it. It was a small wagon pulled by two horses. The man holding the reins was dressed in a large riding coat that covered him protecting him from the weather. The cart was not travelling fast, slow and steady seemed to be the order of the day. Occasionally the driver flicked the reins to encourage the horses that any idea of stopping would not be a good idea. Agnes narrowed her eyes as a sudden flurry of the threatened snow began dropping onto the scene below. She judged the road and the speed of the cart and made her descent landing gently behind a stone wall, in a small copse of trees that lined the road on the outskirts of the town. As she waited for the cart she had time to pick up a number of old sticks and dead branches from the ground and, as the cart approached, she bent herself double and held them tightly to her chest. She began to hobble along the side of the road and by the time the cart approached she was covered in a layer of snow that made her almost invisible. She turned and stepped aside as it drew closer looking closely at the drivers face. Once she was sure he had seen her she raised her hand and a thin reedy voice came out of her mouth. The cart slowed down.

"A lift for an old woman kind sir, the weather is inclement and I have far to go!"

Before the driver could answer her she detected a whispered voice coming from the rear of the wagon from under the cover. Without acknowledging her the driver suddenly whipped the horses and tugged the reins sharply making them speed up. As the cart passed by her he lashed the whip in her direction. Quickly she held the sticks in front of her and the vicious leather end cracked among the dead wood. To create an effect she fell backwards and allowed herself to roll at the side of the road in the gathering snow. The cart plunged forward down the road. As it disappeared she pulled herself to her feet.

"Well that was rude of them!" she thought. Then she remembered the voice from the back of the cart. She wondered who it could have been. The air shimmered and a crow rose back into the air and slowly flapped its way through the falling snow keeping the cart in vision.

Night was falling when the cart came to a stop by a bridge that carried the road over a small moorland stream. She flew low and settled on a dry stone wall some yards away from the stationary cart. She watched as the horses whinnied and stamped their hooves. Their breath came out of their nostrils like jets of steam out of the spout of a boiling kettle.

As she watched the driver got down from his seat, climbed down from the wagon and pulled back the cover to reveal a number of large, square, wooden crates. As she tried to see them more clearly a figure suddenly rose from the back of the wagon. As the driver held out his arm to help the man to the ground Agnes looked very closely at him. He was dark set with a very pale, almost white face. His hair was long so that it hung down his neck reaching to his shoulders. He wore a respectable black suit and a pair of very expensive looking riding boots. If it hadn't have been for the hair the man could have been taken for a member of the professions, a doctor or, given the paleness of his face, an undertaker. The man accepted the hand of the driver and stepped down off the cart. He turned and walked down towards the stream. It was then that Agnes noticed the man was holding his arm awkwardly. She looked closer. His jacket had a ragged tear around the shoulder and blood appeared to be seeping through the cloth. The man reached the stream and squatted on his haunches. He leant forward, scooped up a handful of icy water and began to bathe his wound with it. As the water touched the man body it fizzed and steam drifted into the air. The man repeated the actions twice more before standing up and flexing his damaged arm. As he turned away from the stream and returned to the cart Agnes noticed that not only had the wound healed but the hole in his jacket had also been repaired.

As he climbed back onto the wagon he turned his head in the direction of the crow sitting on the stone wall. For the first time Agnes saw his eyes. They were bright red, pregnant with malice. As their eyes met Agnes felt a jab of panic. The part of her that was crow suddenly found a chink in her thoughts and took over her mind. The bird took off, circled the bridge, and flew off in the opposite direction. Agnes fought hard to try to take back control, but the crow had been so alarmed by the man in black with the red eyes that its natural instinct completely overruled Agnes's will power. It careered across the sky, spinning and tumbling, rising and falling. Eventually the crow tired and fell fluttering onto the ground. Agnes seized the opportunity and regained control of the bird. She cast her mind throughout the crow's body and felt a warmth creep through its flesh. She was back in control. By the time she had found the road and the bridge across the moorland stream the cart and its occupants had long been gone.

She rose in the air and scoured the moorland. There was no sign. She landed by the side of the road. There was a shimmer and an elderly lady appeared standing at the side of the road. She need some thinking time. She moved her arms and a soft glowing light appeared around her. As the snow fell, if you looked very closely, you could see that it never fell near to the glowing lady. In fact the more you looked the more you would swear that the lady was bathed in sunshine.

Insulated from the cold Agnes sat on the wall. From nowhere a hot mug of tea appeared in her hand. Deep down the sight of the man in black with the red eyes had affected her greatly. What she sensed in those eyes was sheer evil. Not only had the man got powers that he had used against her, she realised he knew who she was and the made her very uncomfortable. She sipped her tea and cast her mind back to her earlier visit to "The Merchant". Could be the driver and his passenger be the mysterious servant and master the captain and his mate had spoken about? If it was the case then were the strange square boxes the part of that cargo that made the crew uneasy? Well there was only one way to find out. The elderly lady suddenly disappeared and an owl launched itself off the wall and flew in a direct path to Scarborough.

Chapter Five

Marmaduke opened an eye. His whiskers twitched. He let out a small growl. Something wasn't right. He glanced around the kitchen. The shepherd and his wife had returned to their own cottage. The widow had retired to the privacy of her own grief up in her bedroom. Whitby John sat opposite him, next to the fireplace. His head was on his chest and a series of loud snores drifted out of his open mouth. Marmaduke rolled onto his feet and quietly let himself out of the front door. Outside the snow was falling covering everything with a soft white blanket. His one ear twitched. The sheep were restless. The dogs were lying flat, their heads turning from side to side cocking their heads one way and another. There was a blur and a black shape padded its way across the farmyard. He stopped where Agnes's protective screen met the ground and began a slow and methodical search along the perimeter.

After a few minutes he found what he had been looking for. A hole in the ground. Something had tunnelled under the protective shield. The black shape sniffed the hole, raised its head and bounded across the farmyard. There was movement behind one of the barns. He leapt and landed on all fours. He growled. The figures in front of him froze in terror. Marmaduke growled again, lashed out a paw and the figures cowered back, almost falling over themselves. There was a blur and Marmaduke returned to his human form. Now he could look down on the figures.

"Bejeesus don't be doing things like that!" Said the small figure standing next to him.

Marmaduke bent down to look the little man in the face.

"Boggles!" he said.

"Well, you're observant, I'll give you that." Replied the Boggle.

"What are you doing, and don't try to lie to me!" Although Marmaduke had never met a Boggle before he knew of them by reputation. All Boggles had bad reputations. If anything went missing the disappearance was blamed on Boggles. If a cow caught ill or a horse went lame it was blamed on Boggles. This left the boggles feeling as if they were being made scapegoats. It gave them an inferiority complex that they made up for by stealing anything they could get their hands on. Thus all self perpetuating myths began.

As soon as the Boggle opened its mouth Marmaduke knew it was lying. He bent forward and poked it firmly in the chest with his finger. As he poked he allowed his finger nail to turn into a very sharp claw.

The Boggle looked down at it as it stroked his chest. "Not safe on moor. Safe here!"

Marmaduke looked puzzled. He poked the Boggle in the chest once again.

"Bad things on moor. Chase Boggles, catch Boggles. Never see Boggles again. See witch, see her cast protect spell over farm. We come to farm. Boggles safe."

Marmaduke looked at the rest of the Boggles who were all nodding their heads so violently that some of them lost their hats. He counted them. Twelve, or was it thirteen. Counting had never been his strong point, and the Boggles seemed to be incapable of keeping still.

"Come with me!" He said

The lead Boggle was about to say something but then a claw flicked one of his buttons off his jacket.

As he watched it fly through the air, the lead Boggle nodded.

"Lead on!" It said.

Marmaduke herded them into the farmhouse kitchen, which wasn't easy. Herding Boggles turned out to be remarkably similar to herding cats, impossible. They kept darting here and there. Tripping up, jumping up, running off, and falling over each other. Eventually Marmaduke co-opted the assistance of the two sheep dogs who found the prospect of herding a lot of squealing little men across the farmyard both challenging and ironic. If the sheep dogs could have smiled they would have.

Finally he got them inside the farmhouse, much to the amazement of Whitby John who woke to see a lot of men who, at the most, were only one foot tall. His mood quickly changed from amazement to annoyance as they clambered all over him to get nearer to the fire.

"They are Boggles!" Explained Marmaduke. "They've come under Agnes's protective screen. They are frightened out there on the moor."

Whitby John looked up at Marmaduke. "They burrowed under the shield?" he asked.

Marmaduke nodded. Whitby John shook his head. "I wonder what followed them?" He simply said. He looked up. Marmaduke wasn't there. Through the open door he could make out a dark shape racing across the farmyard.

He saw it as he rounded the corner of the shepherd's cottage. He bounded forward and, with one leap, he jumped and landed on the creatures back, raking it along its sides with his talons. The creature beneath him bucked and writhed, its head turning, its fangs trying to tear at the thing on its back. Marmaduke held on with all four limbs. Then he sank his fangs into the back of the creature's neck. The thing threw its head back and let out a ghastly howl.

Marmaduke leapt off and the air around him shimmered. The creature looked up with blood reddened eyes. It began to froth at the mouth, drool hanging down from its slobbering mouth. Before it could jump Marmaduke fired his pistol. The creature dropped dead at his feet. Marmaduke bent down to examine it. At first glance it seemed to be a very large dog, but no breed of dog was ever born with a mouth and teeth that this creature possessed. The jaw was descended to allow the huge front teeth, designed to rip and tear, freedom to snap and bite. The canine teeth were definitely fangs. Even in death the creature's eyes glowed red. Marmaduke bent down and dragged the body across the farmyard leaving a red bloody trail across the cold white snow.

He knew exactly what he needed to do. He dragged the body to the perimeter of the shield and found the hole made by the Boggles. Unceremoniously he dumped the dogs body into the hole. Using his feet he pushed the corpse deeper and deeper until it would go no further. Half of it was still out of the hole and so he piled loose soil and rocks on it. When he was satisfied he couldn't do any better he stamped on the earth making it tight packed and hard.

When he had satisfied himself that the thing was buried he stood up and sniffed the air around him. A mixture of scents assaulted his nose. Sheep, damp dogs, Boggles and very faintly, almost under the other scents, was a deeply unnatural and offensive smell. He turned his head to the left and to the right. It was the smell of the creature. He followed its trace back to the corner of the shepherd's cottage. Finally he was satisfied that the creature had entered the tunnel under the shield by itself. It was alone. Marmaduke turned and looked toward the bleak moorland. How many more were out there he wondered.

He returned to the farmhouse kitchen to find a hive of activity. Joan, the farmer's wife, woken by the sound of tiny voices and breaking ornaments had rushed downstairs. Unfazed by sight of twelve, or was it thirteen, little men running riot over her home and her belongings, not to mention over Whitby John, was too much. She'd picked up a very handy and very heavy rolling pin, smacked it down hard on the kitchen table and demanded peace.

As Marmaduke entered he found twelve or thirteen Boggles sitting in a line on a settle. They were very quiet. All their eyes were on the very angry woman holding a very large rolling pin. Whitby John looked up. Marmaduke nodded.

"You were right. Something else followed the Boggles through the hole."

The leader of the Boggles looked at Joan and then at Marmaduke. Such was the fear the farmer's wife and her rolling pin had put into him, he actually raise his hand before he spoke.

"Told you. Bad things on moor. Things that follow and chase Boggles." Beside him the other Boggles chattered and nodded their heads.

Marmaduke looked down at him "How many of those creatures are out on the moors?"

The Boggles shook their heads. "Boggles not stay around long enough to count. See one and run. See another run, see another and run again. Boggles don't hang around long enough to ask creature if it the same one we just ran from, or a different one. Boggles just run."

The rest of the Boggles nodded their heads and began a high pitched chant of "Boggles run....Boggles run!"

They stopped when Joan tapped the palm of her hand with the rolling pin. Marmaduke looked out of the window. A mist was covering the farmyard. Streaks of grey were flicking across the sky. Dawn was breaking. He yawned. It had been long night. As he closed his eyes he hoped the protective shield held good in daylight.

Chapter Six

As soon as Agnes arrived home she set to work casting a cloaking spell over her roof and, across the windows and doors. She was both annoyed and puzzled. Whoever or whatever the man in black was, he certainly knew about her. He had appeared in her scrying bowl looking in. She wondered about the dark shape she had seen cross the moon. She experienced a feeling that she was unused to feeling. She felt vulnerable. She needed thinking time. She passed through the cellar wall and sat in her twenty first century cottage. She flicked her finger and her television sprang into life. It was the local news. She watched as a variety of reporters stood in snow showers all over the county reporting road closures. Many schools would not be opening in the morning. Most public transport had stopped. She nodded as Harry Gration told his viewers that no let up was in sight. More snow was forecast to fall. That however wasn't the problem that was uppermost in her mind. Her problem was back in the eighteenth century. Her problem was personal. She flicked her finger and the television turned itself off. She brought to mind the image of the man in black. He was tall, almost good looking. In most company he would appear as a respectable, upright citizen, a member of some gentleman's club, or a patron of the theatre, if it hadn't been for his red eyes and an aura of pure evil that oozed from his body, and he had power. The man could certainly shape shift. She had no doubt that he and the largest black dog she had seen on the moors were one and the same, the wound proved that. Marmaduke had wounded the dog in the shoulder and she had seen for herself that the man carried a wound in the same place. He had healed himself with nothing but a handful of moorland water.

The most worrying aspect of his power though was his ability to see her, to recognise her even when she was housed in the crow's body, and then to cut through her own power to tap into the true nature of the bird. He had bypassed her power and instilled such a fear in the creature that the crow's nature came to the surface. That was very worrying. She needed to prepare herself. She needed to arm herself with some very specialised lotions and potions. With a sigh she pulled herself out of her armchair and walked across the room to her kitchen. She fired up her cooker, pulled her special pan off its shelf and began to search at the back of her cupboards for some very specialised ingredients. It was going to be a long night.

Sometime later as a number of different pots and pans gently simmered and bubbled on her oven she sat back and reflected on another question. Were the boxes from the same cargo that were sat in the hold of "The Merchant" still at anchor in Scarborough Harbour? She wondered whether that was where they were heading.

She stood up and reached for her scrying bowl.

She had half filled it with water when she suddenly threw it down the sink. No! The last time she used the bowl the eyes had found her and appeared in the bowl. If she could see him, he could see her. She didn't want him to see here in the twenty first century. Whatever happened her enemy must never know that Agnes had the ability to pass through time and cellar walls. Whatever, whoever the man was, he had no place here in the twenty first century. He must remain very firmly back in the seventeen hundreds. She waved a hand over the oven. The pots and pans would bubble away safely. She had a wall to walk through.

Once she had filled her bowl and carried it into the living room she added some special powder. She then stood in the middle of the room and used her fingers to weave a web of invisibility around herself. It didn't make her invisible, but it prevented anyone looking in. She hoped it would be effective enough to prevent his eyes from finding her through the scrying bowl.

She cast her view wide and looked down on the small town. The snow had spread a white blanket over the roofs and streets. Few people were about. A couple of hardened drinkers were making their way through the snow covered cobbles to quench their thirst in The Beehive. For good measure she took a peep inside The Three Mariners. Baccy Lad was busy cleaning tankards and wiping down tables. To her knowledge that was the first time that table had ever been wiped since.... well since being new actually. Two or three drinkers sat quietly by the fireside. No one was arguing. She looked behind bar. Sure enough there stood the Widow Pateley, cloth in hand polishing the bar top. Behind her on some tumble down shelves Agnes noticed that all the bottles and glasses shone and glinted. The Three Mariners would never be the same again.

She moved on. "The Merchant" was still in the harbour. Lights shone from the cabin and wheelhouse. Someone was at home. She scanned the harbour side. There was no sign of the cart, its driver, or the man in black.

She moved her hand and the vision cleared. Perhaps she should have a rethink. She had assumed, probably wrongly, that the man in black was taking the boxes across the moor to the ship. Perhaps he wasn't. Perhaps he was taking the boxes off the ship and onto the moor, in which case the boxes on board were waiting to be unloaded. She tutted with annoyance. That meant the man in black was still out on the moor somewhere, and he had some unknown reason for being there. She shook her head. She had no idea what that reason could be.

Before she went to bed she decided to check on the situation up on the farm. She moved her hand and she looked down on the buildings and the yard. She noticed the tracks and the footprints in the snow. Then she saw the body of the black dog, half in and half out of the tunnel entrance. Then she gave herself a good kicking. She hadn't thought to extend the protection underground. She closed her eyes and concentrated very hard. Within minutes she had rectified her mistake. Then she took to wondering what could have burrowed the tunnel in the first place. She took a look inside the buildings. On one side of the yard the shepherd lay asleep in his bed. In the next room his wife was attending to one of the children that had woken with a fright.

She moved across to the farmhouse where her eyes opened wide with surprise. Below her she could see Whitby John seated in front of the glowing fire, wrapped up in a blanket. In the opposite chair sat Marmaduke. His feet were up on the fender and his arms crossed above his chest. Both of them were trying to sleep and failing. The reason why they couldn't sleep was obvious. All around them, and in some cases on them, were a number of tiny men. She couldn't count them as they wouldn't stay still long enough. They were on the furniture, under the furniture, one was climbing the curtains, others seemed to be running back and forth, in and out of the kitchen. She took a peek inside. Joan the farmer's widow was busy pouring out very small measures of fresh milk. A newly made loaf was cut up into tiny slices each covered thickly with butter. She waved her hand and the vision disappeared. She sighed. As if she didn't have enough problems to worry about, now she had Boggles. A more infuriating, annoying creature had never been created. Unpredictable and mischievous. She smiled. She quite liked Boggles.

As she went to bed she reminded herself t take a walk down the harbour first thing. She wanted to know more about the ship in the harbour. She knew a man who, if he didn't know himself, would be able to find out. The first thing she would do would be to pay a visit to Andrew Marks and his chandlery.

Chapter Seven

The smell of frying bacon woke Marmaduke up. When he opened his eyes he rubbed them in disbelief. Sat at the table were the Boggles but that wasn't the surprise. The surprise was that they all sat still, all with their heads pointing in the direction of the kitchen from where the sound and smell of frying bacon was emanating. He stood up and walked across the room and found an empty seat. He looked up as Whitby John came in from the back door carrying a bucket of water.

The breakfast was excellent. Fat rashers of bacon and fried eggs filled his plate. A mug of steaming tea washed it down. As he licked his lips Marmaduke thought he'd better tale a look around the farm and check the magical protection. He pushed his empty plate away and left the farmhouse.

Outside the snow had settled during the night and laid another two inches deep carpet over everything. There were no fresh tracks in the snow. Nothing seemed to have entered. He walked across to the tunnel. The body of the dog still lay where he had pushed it, half in and half out of the tunnel entrance. As he approached the body his nostrils were assaulted by a very bad smell. It came from the carcass of the dog. He shook his head. A smell that bad should only emanate from a body verging on purification and the creature hadn't been dead that long. He brushed the snow from it. The creature was in the final stages of decay. In fact the more Marmaduke looked the more the creature seemed to be decaying in front of his eyes. He sat back on his haunches and watched.

It took over half an hour for the creature's body to completely rot away. At the end there wasn't even a bone left. It was as if the body had just dissolved. He scratched his head. Now the tunnel was unblocked. He looked around and found some lose stones and old straw piled up behind a stone wall. He spent the next hour using the material to block up the hole. By the time he had finished there was no trace that the creature had ever existed. He was stamping the ground flat when he heard it. It was a sound that could only be described as a howl. It made the hair on the back of his head rise. His whiskers twitched. With one bound he made it back to the farmhouse. Inside the occupants had also heard the sound. Whitby John and Joan had bolted the back door. The Boggles were less constructive. They were panicking, running all over the room in a vain attempt to hide. Three of them were trying to get into a drawer in the dresser. They had pulled it out too far and it could no longer hold their weight. It crashed to the ground almost flattening four more Boggles who were trying to squeeze under the dresser. Everyone froze as Marmaduke closed the door behind him.

"Whatever it is it won't get through Agnes's protection!" he said

"They did!" replied Whitby John nodding in the direction of two Boggles who were trying to hide behind his legs.

Marmaduke nodded. The man had a point. He made a decision. "Stay here. Lock up."

Then he remembered the shepherd. "Wait! Fetch the shepherd and his family. Put the children upstairs." He gave a slight smile. "Let them play with the Boggles."

He could hear the objections and squeals of protest from the small men all across the farmyard.

Once everyone was in the house and the doors securely locked and bolted Marmaduke walked to the perimeter of the magic shield. He stood and looked at where the shield was. If no one could get in could he get out? Well he'd find a way out. He ran, took a leap, and landed on the moor beyond. As he passed through the shield he felt a slight tingle, nothing more. He turned and looked back at the small farm. Everything looked normal, just his footprints in the snow leading to a stone wall. The air shimmered and a giant black cat like shape bounded across the fallen snow and onto the top of the open moor.

The morning was cold and crisp. The sun was trying to shed some warmth on the earth below. At least it had stopped snowing. Marmaduke stopped when he entered a small wood that lay at the head of a narrow valley down which a stream trickled between the overhanging grasses and snow. He almost missed it at first. The creature was stooped down on all fours lapping at the icy water. At first glance Marmaduke mistook it for a boulder. That was until the creature turned its head showing a pair of bright red eyes. Marmaduke froze. The creature lifted its head and pulled its lips back in a low snarl that revealing a large reddened mouth with a tongue that lolled and drooped over a set of very large and very pointed fangs.

Marmaduke snarled back showing his own fangs which, whilst not as numerous, were just as impressive.

Without warning the creature leapt forward snarling and snapping. Marmaduke leapt up and landed on the lower branches of the tree he happened to be standing under. The creature stopped, looked up at the giant cat in the tree and let out a howl. Marmaduke was wondering how high the creature could jump when he heard another howl. It came from further down the valley. Then he heard a second reply. This came from across the open moor. Marmaduke sighed. This could prove tricky. The air shimmered. Before the creature could react the giant cat turned into a human, and a human with a gun in its hand. There was an explosion. Then nothing.

Marmaduke looked down at the base of the tree. He had shot the creature right between the eyes.

The creature fell dead among the snow and the tree

roots. Marmaduke listened, cocking his head one way and another. Something was moving through the wood and heading in his direction. He pulled out his second pistol and aimed it towards the ground. He heard the creature stop some way away. He tried to see through the branches and snow, but couldn't see the creature to take a shot at it. Then the creature let out another howl. It was answered almost immediately, this time from behind him. Then a third howl sounded, some way away in another direction. He gripped the trunk of the tree to steady himself. There were three of them out there. He slid his pistol back into his belt whilst he began to reload the one he had just discharged. He sniffed the air and sensed movement. The three creatures were now circling him, getting closer and closer to the tree he was in with every turn. Then there was a growl. One of the creatures noticed the body at the base of the tree. It let out a long wail which was picked up buy the other two. Marmaduke finished loading his pistol and drew the other. Bracing himself with his back to the trunk he held both pistols towards the ground, just waiting for an opportunity to see the creatures in the undergrowth. He remained stationary for a few minutes. Below him the only sound he could hear was that of the creature's heavy breathing. He looked closer. There was a small cloud of steaming breath coming from a bush down to his right. He took aim and was about to fire when the silence was broken by a distant high pitched whistle. It was so high that if he hadn't been half cat he wouldn't have heard it at all. The effect on the creatures below was immediate. They rose from their hiding places and, without a backwards look at the tree where their prey was hiding, they turned and raced out of the wood and across the open moor.

When he was sure they weren't coming back Marmaduke dropped back to the ground. The air shimmered and the shape of a giant cat bounded across the landscape in pursuit of the three large dogs. It wasn't easy trying to follow their tracks across the moor as their paw prints were lost in the snow that was between the heather and the small gullies that ran across the moor. Eventually he reached the crest of a small hill that marked the top of the moor. He looked to his right and then to his left. Nothing. He sniffed the air. There was a feint smell. A distant movement caught his eye. A mile away, halfway down a small hill, a man was driving a horse and cart along a small road that cut across the moorland. Marmaduke immediately thought of the fate of the farmer and his cart. He was about to take chase and give warning but something made him stop. The cart was heading off the open moor. Soon it would be down among the fields and head towards the main road. He stayed where he was and scanned the surrounding landscape. The cart and the horse were the only things moving. The three creatures had completely disappeared. He decided he should return to the farm. There was always the possibility the creatures could have doubled back. The black shape bounded across the moor until he reached the head of the valley where the farm lay. Everything looked normal as he bounded towards it.

The effect of running into the protective shield was very similar to the effect of running at full speed into a very high and very solid brick wall. He sat up in the snow and bracken and felt his face to see if his nose was broken. It wasn't, though one of his fangs had a chip in it. He let out a small low groan. He could run out of the protected area, but such was the nature of Agnes's protective shield, that he couldn't run back into it. He stood up and brushed himself down. He knew that walking around it, hoping to find flaws in it was a waste of time, but he began to walk anyway.

Chapter Eight

The morning was bright and crisp. It had stopped snowing and Agnes walked carefully through the old streets trying not to slip on the snow and ice. She made it to the top of Custom House Steps and stepped aside as a group of fishermen walked up in the opposite direction. As they passed her each gave her a nod of respect. She was nodding back when two of them took her by her arms and, despite her protestations, led her carefully down to the bottom of the stairs and then ran back up laughing all the way. Sometimes there were disadvantages to this "being old thing" she thought to herself.

She was still trying to work out whether she had just been helped, or had been patronised, or was the victim of a joke as she walked into Andrew Marks chandlery. He was about to show her into his office when she shook her head and indicated she wanted to speak with him outside. He went to the door where Agnes held his arm and led him across the road to the side of the harbour. She pointed out to where "The Merchant" was still tied up at the dockside.

"What can you tell me about that ship?" She said as she pointed down the dock

Andrew looked in the direction in which she was pointing. There were at least a dozen ships out there. He was about to turn when Agnes hissed in his ear.

"The Merchant. Four down on the right."

He looked again. He thought he recognised it but couldn't be sure. There were hundreds of ships just like the one she had pointed to plying their business up and down the coast, not to mention others that made the regular journey across the North Sea to Germany, Denmark, Holland and as far north as

Norway. He looked again. There was something about the name. A slight bell was ringing at the back of his head. He nodded towards Agnes. He had seen enough. Back in his office he pulled out a large leather bound ledger, opened it and flicked through the pages. Then he stopped and ran his finger down the page. There it was "The Merchant. He carried the ledger across the office and placed it open on his desk. He was a bit peeved when he realised Agnes had sat in his best office chair. He perched himself on the edge of his desk and pulled the ledger in front of Agnes. She looked down. The page contained the names of ships and lists of cargo. Some were in one colour, others in another. She looked up at Andrew.

"I remembered the name. A couple of years ago it came here and tried to off load some dubious gin."

He turned a couple of pages and pointed to another entry. "Here, the same ship. Came in with a load of wool."

Agnes raised her head.

Andrew continued. "The wool was fine, best quality. The trouble was that it was wrapped around kegs of the finest French brandy. They are chancers. They run the ship up and down the coast, taking whatever cargo they can get and anything else on the side. If they have a hold full of coal they'd have something hidden underneath it. Chancers!"

Agnes looked up at Andrew. "I don't suppose you know what she's carrying now do you?"

Andrew shook his head. "I didn't even know she was in the harbour. Someone's getting a bit slack out there."

Agnes smiled. "I thought you had eyes and ears on every capstan." She said.

Andrew smiled. "I have a man or two, just to keep an eye on the comings and goings."

Agnes shook her head. "Well someone's not doing their job. The ships been there for the best part of three, maybe four days now."

At that news Andrews face fell. "It can't have. I'd have heard by now! Excuse me."

He suddenly left the office and closed the door behind him. From inside the office Agnes could hear Andrew firing questions at his staff.

He came back grim faced. "No one's seen hide nor hair of him for the last three days."

Agnes felt a sinking feeling in the pit of her stomach.

It took the best part of an hour with a scrying bowl cobbled together with an old piece of silver plate before they found the body. It was lying at the bottom of the harbour, weighted down with a pile of old chains. Andrew was genuinely shocked, and upset. Agnes poured him a glass of his own finest French brandy. As he took a sip she looked at him.

"Did he have family?"

Andrew shook his head. "He usually dossed down at the Seaman's Mission, picked up odd jobs here and there. He kept an eye out for me. He wasn't a bad fellow. Had a thing about strong drink. He was reliable though!"

"But missing for three days?" Agnes said pointedly.

Andrew took another sip of brandy. "Not uncommon if there's nothing to report."

He looked towards the closed door towards the shop. "Mind you someone out there should have noticed. The man was always popping in for the loan of a coin, on account like. He usually spent it in the Dog and Duck."

Agnes nodded. She had already formed a pretty accurate picture of the deceased.

Andrew placed his glass carefully on the desk. "I take it that his death and you asking after that ship is no coincidence?"

Agnes shook her head. "Someone on that boat doesn't want anyone knowing what's on board, and will go to any lengths. I fear your man on the pier might have seen something he shouldn't have."

Andrew shook his head. "Those two are chancers. A bit here, a bit there. Killing a man who saw their cargo is well out of their league."

Agnes shook her head. "They might be, but what about them whose paying them? That's the ones I'm interested in. They wouldn't hesitate to kill. They already have."

Andrew raised an eyebrow and Agnes decided to tell him the whole story. She began with the dead sheep on the moor and didn't stop until Andrew himself came into the story.

"The rest you know!" She finished and refilled his glass once more. He took a deep drink and carefully placed the glass back on his desk. He looked up.

"I take it you want a watch kept on the vessel." He said.

Agnes nodded once more. "If it's not too much trouble."

Andrew shook his head. "It's no trouble, no trouble at all. In fact I was going to do it myself."

His face took on a serious look, lines formed across his forehead and a vein stood out on his neck. He looked far away into the distance as he spoke. "This is personal. No one comes into my harbour and kills one of my men without ramifications. A rat won't be able to get aboard that ship without me knowing its name and next of kin!"

He lifted his glass and drained it on one gulp. "In fact that ship just might not leave the harbour."

He reached for the bottle but Agnes placed her hand over the top of the glass. Andrew looked up at her. She looked back straight into his eyes. "Be careful Andrew. I've no idea who or what we're dealing with here, but whatever it is it's dangerous. It is evil. Don't do anything without telling me first!"

She reached into one of her pockets and pulled out a small oval stone. She slid it across the desk. Andrew looked down at it. She pushed it further towards him. "Take it. When you need me just hold it tight in one hand and think of me. No need to do anything else. Just hold and think. I'll be there as soon as possible."

After she left Andrew picked up the stone and resisting the temptation to hold and squeeze it, placed it into his waistcoat pocket. He spent the next hour calling in favours. By the middle of the afternoon he had eyes and ears all over the harbour, all of them looking towards The Merchant".

Chapter Nine

After leaving Andrew Agnes made her way home where she picked up a small bag, filled it with her specially made lotions and potions, placed the bag across her shoulders, and walked out into her yard. The air shimmered and a seagull rose into the air and flapped its way gracefully over the town towards the moors.

She was halfway to the farmhouse, enjoying the cool crisp morning and the gentle breeze, allowing the pale sun to warm her and the breeze to lift her, allowing her to glide when she felt a sudden and very hard thump on the centre of her back. Before she could react she felt a tearing of her wing. She allowed the seagull to twist and turn in the air. As it spun she realised that the gull was being attacked by three large black birds. At first she thought they were crows, and then she noticed their eyes. They were bright red. She allowed the gull to drop through the air and she swooped across the moor. The red eyed crows followed her, snapping at her with their beaks and tearing at her feathers with their talons. She turned once again but a gust of wind caught her by surprise and blew her sideways, right into the path of one of the birds. It ripped her wing, pulling out feathers and damaging the tendons that controlled its flight. Agnes felt a jolt of pain scream through the body of the gull. It tried to use the wing but nothing happened. It began to spiral towards the moor below. As she fell Agnes spotted the three birds. They were circling overhead waiting for her to crash. She concentrated all her thoughts and tried to control the flight of the seagull. She gained control but too late. She hit the moor with a sickening crash.

It was the snow and the heather that saved her from serious damage. As the gull lay tangled up in the heather she forced it to remain very, very still. She let out a small move of her good wing and a slight mist appeared rolling over the top of the moor. As it passed over the top of the seagull the air shimmered and an adder slid between the sprigs of heather until it found the hard ground. Then it slithered away. She found refuge under a loose rock and curled up. She allowed her mind to drift beyond the mind of the snake and float up above the rock. Overhead the three black birds were still circling over the spot where the seagull fell. She waited. Eventually the crows must have been satisfied that the gull would not rise up again and they flew off. She watched until they appeared as tiny dots and then finally disappeared. The air shimmered and an elderly lady was sitting on a rock in the middle of the moor. She looked down at her left arm. There was blood oozing through the cuts and the rips in the sleeve of her dress. She concentrated and the bleeding stopped. She examined her damaged arm. She would need some stitches.

The attack had shaken her. She knew that crows frequently attacked seagulls, but she also knew that they weren't ordinary crows. They had red eyes and instead of claws, talons! She needed to get to the farm. The air shimmered and the elderly woman disappeared. In her place perching on top of the rock was a peregrine falcon, the fastest bird in the English skies. It rose in the air and flew off in the direction of the farm.

She approached the buildings from a height and was just about to swoop down into the farmyard when she spotted a figure sat on a wall just outside her protective shield. It was Marmaduke. She swooped down and landed on the wall next to him. The air shimmered. Marmaduke turned his head to find Agnes sat next to him.

"I can't get back in!" He said. Then he noticed her damaged arm.

"What happened?" he asked showing concern.

She turned to him. "Come on. I'll explain on the way to the farmhouse."

She hopped off the wall and signalled for Marmaduke to follow her. As she approached her shield she took hold of Marmaduke's hand. Despite his belief in her powers Marmaduke braced himself as he approached the shield, but nothing happened. They just walked straight through it as if it wasn't there. He made no pretence of even trying to understand her magic so he never even bothered to wonder how. He just accepted that that was the way things were. Anyway his nose still hurt.
The two of them passed through the shield and walked onto the farmhouse.

As soon as she entered the living room she was surrounded by Boggles. They ran around her pulling at her skirts and jumping up and down to attract her attention. They bounced on and over the furniture, one climbed up the curtains. Agnes clapped her hands and they fell still. She shooed them and they all made a dive to sit on the settee. There was some squabbling and a bit of hair pulling before they all sat in a quiet neat row, swinging their legs backwards and forwards. Whitby John had noticed Agnes's arm as soon as she entered the room and, as the Boggles settled down, he stood up and led her to his chair. She sat down heavily and told her story. When she had finished everyone remained silent.

She turned to Marmaduke. "How did you come to be outside the shield?" She asked.

Now it was Marmaduke's turn to tell of his adventures earlier in the day. Agnes listened carefully, stopping his flow every so often to ask questions.

She let out a sigh when he finished the tale. "Evil black dogs, mysterious strangers, a ship with an unknown cargo, a dead man in the harbour, and killer crows!"

She turned to Joan who, having seen the state of Agnes's arm had appeared with a clean cloth and a bowl of hot water. "I'm so sorry that all this had befallen you." Agnes said.

The widow wiped her eyes with the sleeve of her dress and let out a deep sob "He's still out there!"

At first Agnes thought the woman was talking about the man in black with the red eyes, then the penny dropped. She was talking about her husband.

Agnes lent forward and patted the woman's arm. "I'm so sorry. What with everything else I had forgotten. Tomorrow we will visit the vicar and arrange for a funeral in three days time."

As she spoke Agnes allowed the woman to bathe her torn arm. She felt the warm water sting as it touched her wound. Agnes knew she could attend to herself, in fact she preferred to heal herself, but right at this moment the farmer's widow needed something to concentrate her mind. At the mention of the funeral everyone fell silent, even the Boggles who had no idea of what or who was being talked about.

Once Joan had tied a bandage around Agnes's arm Agnes looked around. "We need a plan. There are things that need to be attended to. We need an undertaker and the body transporting to the church."

Marmaduke spoke up. "The only problem is that, at the very least, there are three of those creatures out there. Whatever our red-eyed man is about he seems to be doing it on the moors. It's not safe out there."

Agnes flexed her bandaged arm. "Well, we'd better make it safe. We have a funeral to arrange."

She patted Joan's arm and gave her a special look. Although it didn't take away her grief the woman felt strangely comforted.

Agnes stood up. "Marmaduke and I need some thinking time. We'll be back soon. In the meanwhile, Whitby John, I'd be grateful if you could do what needs to be done around here." She looked over at the Boggles and gave them a look. They all shrank back. "You can help as well!"

Seeing the look on her face they all began nodding as fast as their heads could move. As she left the room Agnes turned to them all. "The protection will hold. It is strong. Do not leave its safety. Remember, whatever you see out there cannot get in."

Once outside she led Marmaduke to an old broken seat. She flicked a finger and the snow melted from it. They sat and Marmaduke was surprised to find the seat was warm. Agnes lent forward.

"This isn't going to be as easy as I made it sound. Whoever or whatever is out there knows about us. It knows we have certain talents. It has attacked me as an owl, a crow and as a seagull. It has seen me scrying. It has been watching us and it knows where we live."

She sighed and added "This is going to be tricky."

Marmaduke scratched his head. "I'm still puzzled as to why they ran off at the sound of the whistle, and who blew it."

Agnes rocked slightly. "They had to run. It was their master calling. Those creatures are under tight control. They do as they are ordered to, as they are trained to do. Despite having their quarry at their mercy, they had to leave."

Marmaduke looked up. "That means that our man in black is their master."

"He's the pack leader." Replied Agnes.

"But where did they get to? There was no sign of

them on the moor."

Agnes looked across the farmyard and out to the open moor. "I think the man in the cart you saw was him. They ran to him."

Marmaduke shook his head. "Can't have. I'd have seen them when I saw the cart. There was no sign of them, they just weren't there."

Agnes turned to look at him. "Suppose they were in the cart?"

Marmaduke thought. It was possible. "In the cart!" he mused.

Agnes placed her head on her temple. She felt a vibration that stretched from her neck to her forehead. "We've got to get to Andrew. He's calling, something's wrong!"

The air shimmered and a very large peregrine falcon flexed its wings and took off. In seconds it was a dot in the sky. At the same time a black cat like shape bounded across the farmyard and disappeared into the surrounding moorland.

Chapter Ten

The peregrine falcon skirted the headland on which Scarborough Castle was built. As it skimmed across the rock face a thousand kittiwakes took flight alarmed by the sight of the bird of prey. The falcon ignored the sea birds and fell to the ground behind one of the many sheds that lined the shore line and harbour, sheds that housing fishing equipment, timber merchants, carpenters, net makers and all the other auxiliary trades and crafts that supplied the needs of the small port and its shiping. As soon as Agnes stepped onto the harbour side she could see a commotion. A large crowd had gathered halfway down the pier where "The Merchant" was moored. They seemed to be standing in a semi circle in the centre of which was a group of men. As she walked towards them the crowd parted. A murmur went around the people who nudged each other, nodded and pointed towards her. She tried to ignore it, she hated being the centre of attention.

She considered using a cloaking spell and then smiled to herself as she thought of the commotion and general brouhaha that would break out if she suddenly disappeared in front of their eyes. She would never be able to walk down her street again.

As she approached the group she realised they were excise men holding drawn pistols that were pointing towards a ship tied up on the side of the dock. It was "The Merchant". At first she wondered if they had discovered the illicit sherry. Her wondering was brought to a quick end when Andrew ran up to her.

"There's been an incident!" he said simply.

Agnes considered saying something about stating the obvious but resisted a sarcastic reply. The man was obviously deeply concerned about something. She looked over to the side of the dock and then noticed that the Captain and the First Mate were standing looking down at their own ship. Both were nursing wounds. The Fist Mate was holding his bloodied arm through a shredded jacket sleeve. The Captain had a deep tear in his leg. Some people were attending to their injuries.

She turned back to Andrew. He pointed to a man at the front of the crowd. "He is one of my men, keeping an eye on the ship. Go ask him."

Agnes walked up to the man. "What happened?"

The man looked to see an elderly woman speaking to him. He was about to tell her to go away when he noticed her eyes. They seemed to engulf him. Then he found himself telling her everything he knew.

He had been watching the ship when a strange noise came out of the hold. The man swore that he heard growling. He was still listening when the sound changed to that of screaming and a lot of crashing and shouting. As he watched the Captain and the First Mate rushed out of the entrance to the hold and, stopping only to bar the hatch behind them, they leapt ashore. It just happened that three excise men were passing and seeing the strange behaviour of "The Merchants" crew grew suspicious.

Currently they were standing ashore debating which one of their number should go aboard to investigate. None of them seemed over keen and the stand-off had lasted the best part of half an hour.

As the man told his tale the growling and snarling from inside the ships hold had grown and was now augmented by the sound of claws scratching and tearing at the hatchway.

Agnes knew what was making that noise. There were black dogs loose in the ships hold. She marched across to the injured crew. Without any introductions she looked the Captain straight in the face and gave him one of her looks.

"Where did the dog come from?" She asked.

The Captain shook his head. "No idea missus!"

She tried another tack. "How many boxes were in the hold?"

The First Mate answered. "Half a dozen left. He took the rest a couple of days ago."

Agnes turned to Andrew who had walked up behind her. "About time your man disappeared. Things could get a bit tricky."

She turned back to the Captain. "How many crates did you ship in total?"

"Twenty five." he replied.

Behind them there was a crashing sound and a gasp from the crowd. A shot rang out.

She moved to the edge of the pier and looked down

onto "The Merchant". A hole had appeared in the side of the hold. Through the jagged and torn wooden planking she could see the shape of a large dogs head. It was snarling and its eyes glowed red as its fangs ripped at the woodwork. A second shot rang out. This time the creature yelped and the head disappeared back into the darkness of the hold.

She turned to Andrew. "Call the troops down. There could be six of them in there."

Andrew didn't need telling twice. He ran into the crowd, grabbed a man by the shoulder and spoke urgently in his ear. The man turned and ran towards the road leading to the Castle.

As Andrew turned to walk back to Agnes he felt someone next to him. He turned. Marmaduke was standing next to him breathing heavily. They walked back to Agnes together.

As they approached Marmaduke noticed that Agnes was moving her finger in a series of fast intricate patterns. He looked down at a ship that had a hole in the side of its cargo hold. As he looked the hole simply disappeared. The planking and the ripped wood had reformed and returned to normal. From inside the hold he heard a howl. It was joined by two others.

Behind him he heard the crowd mutter and murmur and the sound of lots of feet shuffling backwards. The excise men remained where they were, still holding their pistols towards the ship. They seemed unsure of what was happening, or what to do next and cast anxious looks at each other.

Agnes moved her fingers and a slight blue glow appeared and disappeared almost as quickly. She turned to Marmaduke.

"That will hold them."

Marmaduke cocked his one good eye asking the question without saying the words. He wondered if Agnes had intended a very bad pun. He looked but her face gave nothing away.

She turned to one of the excise men. "Trust me, they won't get out."

The man looked at her and shuffled his feet. "That's good, especially as we have to inspect the hold."

Agnes raised an eyebrow. "Is there duty on large black dogs?" She asked.

The excise man shook his head. "There will be duty to pay on what they are guarding. No one has guard dogs without having something worth guarding."

Agnes nodded. The man made sense. His only mistake was in realising that the cargo was the dogs themselves. Six of them in the hold, and another twenty out on the moors. She felt a little shudder down her spine.

She came back to the present as she felt Marmaduke's arm on her arm. Behind her she heard the crowd gasp. She looked up to see a flock of crows plunge down from the sky and begin flapping and pecking and scratching at the heads of the people in the crowd. Four crows made a line for the excise men. The crowd turned and knocked each other over in an attempt to escape under cover inside buildings and sheds, anywhere with a roof. The excise men threw their arms over their heads to protect themselves from the pecking and tearing.

Suddenly there was a loud crack. It was the sound of twenty muskets being fired in a volley. Above them crows stopped in mid flight and dropped like stones onto the pier and into the water of the harbour. A second volley diminished the flock of crows even further. After the third volley the remaining crows took flight and disappeared into the sky.

Agnes looked across to where the shots had been fired. Thank God for the army she thought. The officer in charge saluted and walked towards her. She watched his approach. Lieutenant Smalls still walked with a pronounced limp, injured during enemy action, the citation pronounced. Thrown off his horse was the truth. At least it would add to his military pension when he retired. He stopped in front of Agnes and saluted her once again.

"Stop it!" she said.

Behind him the crowd began to emerge from their hiding places. As they compared their cuts and bruises they looked at the ground. There was no sign of any dead crows. The crowd murmured and then fell to arguing among themselves.

"Typical!" She murmured to herself.

She turned back as Marmaduke and Andrew tried to explain to a confused Lieutenant what was happening. Agnes left them to it and walked across to look down at the ship once more. Despite her magic shield the dogs were far from remaining quiet. By the movement of the ship she figured that they must be stalking side to side in the hold. The ship rocked some more. She wondered if they could be working together to capsize it. She moved her fingers and a sand bank appeared in the harbour where a sand bank had never been before. It gathered beneath "The Merchant" and rose until the ship was held firmly in its grip. The ship stopped swaying and the howling began once again.

"Those things can think!" She said aloud, then a thought struck her. "Unless...."

She whirled around and scanned the crowd and nudged Marmaduke. "He's here somewhere. He's watching. He's controlling the dogs!"

Marmaduke scanned the crowd. As he turned his head he felt Agnes's hand on his shoulder.

"Don't look straight away. At the far end of the harbour, just before the slipway. There's a horse and cart. That's our man!"

Before Marmaduke could react two shots rang out in quick succession. The crowd screamed and ran in all directions. The troopers lifted their muskets looking for a target. There was a shout from along the pier. They looked up to see the Captain and his mate slumped on the ground. Blood pumped from the holes had appeared in their chests. Agnes looked back at the cart. It had disappeared. She turned to the Lieutenant.

"A cart was standing at the far end of the harbour. That's your man."

The Lieutenant didn't need a second telling. As fast as he could he walked across the pier shouting orders as he went. Muskets at the ready the troopers ran off to intercept the cart and its driver.

Agnes turned to the excise men. "Right, let's go and sort that hold out!"

They looked at her as if she had gone mad. She moved her hands in the direction of the ship and nodded. Marmaduke made a leap from the dockside and landed on the ship deck.

Agnes turned to the excise men. "Go on then, go and do what you do best!"

Very carefully the excise men edged forward. Marmaduke sighed. So much for backup. He lent back and gave a mighty kick. The hatch to the hold burst inwards. He stepped back and peered inside. At the far end of the hold he could see six large crates. Three of thee were unopened. The other three had their lids pulled to one side. In front of them lay three very large black dogs. They were fast asleep, breathing heavily, their jaws snapping revealing large evil looking fangs in a red, drooling, slobbering mouth.

"There will be another three in the unopened boxes" Said Agnes and then added, "I've no idea what to do with them!"

After some consultation with the excise men it was agreed that the three sleeping black dogs would be put back into the empty boxes which would then be sealed up. Then all six boxes would be taken from the ship and locked away in the vaults underneath the bonded warehouse. To make sure they were safe, once they were underground Agnes would cast a special seal over them, although she wouldn't mention that to anyone.

Once the crowd had decided that the excitement was over for the day they began to drift back to their work, or to the bar rooms of the dockside inns and taverns to talk over and then argue about what they had just witnessed.

As Agnes and Marmaduke watched the crates being unloaded the Lieutenant marched up behind them. "Lost the bounder!"

Agnes raised an eyebrow. The Lieutenant shook his head. "Don't ask how."

"He's heading back to the moors." Agnes replied.

The Lieutenant looked down. "We tried to cover all roads out of town, but he was ahead of us."

"The moors!" repeated Agnes. "It's the only place he can go. He's transported twenty five crates there already. He's lost six and he's lost his ship. There's no reason for him to come back here. Whatever his purpose be, the answer lies up on the moors."

Lieutenant Smalls was an intelligent officer, that's why Agnes liked him. He thought ahead, he understood ramifications. "I'll inform the Commander right away. We'll send some patrols out. Giant dogs and murderers who attack people with crows, oh he'll love this!"

Agnes sighed. "Tell him to be careful. Those dogs are killers. Three of them would eat a patrol for breakfast. They would be among your men before they knew what hit them. We need more information before we start running all over the moors.

The Lieutenant looked at Agnes and gave a slight shrug of his shoulders. "You know the Commander. He'll get himself involved. He won't be able to help himself."

Agnes nodded. Of course he will. The Lieutenant was right, the Commander wouldn't be able to help himself. "Hang on here for a little while. I'm sure there's something you and your men need to double check. Once we've got this lot under lock and key I'll join you. We'll go see the Commander together."

An hour later Agnes, Marmaduke, Andrew and the Lieutenant were seated around a large table in the Commanders office. The Commander was busy spreading out a large map of the area. He had managed to hold the corners down with a decanter of whiskey, an ink well and a pistol. He was now looking around for something else when Agnes reached into her pocket and pulled out a rather attractive green glass paperweight. She placed it on the fourth corner. The Commander harrumphed, the Lieutenant tried not to smile, and failed.

Agnes looked down at the map. She traced the roads and visualised the landscape. She located the farmstead and from nowhere a small wooden stick with a flag attached appeared on its location. Everyone around the table blinked. They wouldn't have been so surprised had they visited the twenty first century and experienced cocktail sausages, or eaten a piece of pineapple and cheese from a cocktail stick. In the eighteenth century a cocktail stick was a mystery.

"That's the farmstead!" Agnes stated.

Marmaduke pointed a finger with a very large and very pointed nail at another spot on the map. "That's where I saw the cart!" he said.

He traced the nail down the road marked on the map. "That's where they stopped and attacked me."

Two more cocktails sticks appeared on the map.

As Agnes placed the cocktail sticks the Commander noticed that she was wearing a bandage on her arm. He was about to say something when he saw Marmaduke shake his head. The Commander bit his tongue and found himself wondering if the half man half cat creature had learned to read minds.

The Lieutenant was tracing out a series of routes on the map. He became aware that the Commander was watching him. "Sir if we assume that in each sighting the cart continued in the direction it was travelling in."

They all stopped what they were thinking and tried to understand what the Lieutenant was trying to achieve.

"Look!" He said and traced a route out on the map. Then he traced out a second route. Both routes travelled from different directions, but intersected at a cross roads on the top of the moors.

"Where is that?" she asked.

The Commander lifted a magnifying glass and peered at the spot. "Something called Ralph's Cross." He said.

"I think we need to take a closer look at Ralphs Cross" Said Agnes.

The Lieutenant straightened himself up. "We could have a patrol out there inside three hours." He said.

Agnes shook her head. Over by the window was a large platter that was holding some apples. Agnes walked up to it, helped herself to an apple and picked up the dish. She walked back to the table and placed it in the centre of the map. She then made a move over the empty platter with her hand and slowly it filled with water. She pulled out a handful of herbs from her pocket and scattered them over the water. Then, as she was the centre of attention, and she couldn't help herself, she added a little flash and a pop.

She had added too much pop she thought to herself as the Commander, who in his eagerness to see into the water, leapt backwards with singed eyebrows.

"Funny!" said Andrew, "I thought it was the cat that was killed by curiosity!"

That comment earned him a very stern look from Marmaduke.

Agnes passed her hand over the water and an image of the open moor appeared. At its centre was a large and ancient stone cross. She moved her hand and the image shifted. Now she could see the crossroads. Which way she thought to herself.

"One way leads to the main Pickering Turnpike, the other goes deeper into the moors. Seems to peter out in a small valley" It was the voice of Lieutenant Smalls. He had traced the position of both routes on the map.

Agnes switched her view to the road that ran deeper into the moors. She followed it to the head of a small valley. Half way down the valley was a small clump of trees. Behind the trees was a small house. She looked at it. It was well built with windows and a stout door. She moved her hands and the image grew closer. There was smoke drifting out of the chimney. It was occupied.

The water in the dish suddenly shook and splashed over its sides. As it settled the only thing that could be seen was a pair of red staring eyes. Everyone heard the snarl. It echoed around the room. Agnes quickly moved her hand and the water simply disappeared. She looked around the room. For once the four men were silent.

Agnes at down and rubbed her arm. For some reason it had begun to throb. She thought hard and sent a warm glow down her arm to settle and sooth her wound. The quiet was broken by all four men deciding to speak at the same time.

Agnes lifted up her hand. "Gentlemen, we know where he is."

"He also knows where we are!" Exclaimed Andrew.

"He already knew" Said Marmaduke.

"He didn't know about me!" Andrew retorted.

Agnes looked up at him. "He saw you on the dockside. Oh yes, you can bet anything you want, he knew you had spies on the harbour. He's seen us all before. No gentlemen, we win that particular bout. We've gained some knowledge."

The Commander gave his singed eyebrows a rub. His experience of scrying hadn't been enjoyable. Just another reason he disliked magic.

"Surround the bounder. Get a ring of troops around the house. Close in!"

Agnes nodded. "At some point we may have to resort to that. However did anyone see any crates? No matter what you did you couldn't fit twenty five crates into that house. May I remind you he has crates that have the dogs inside them, and I have a very nasty feeling that they are scattered all over the moors. By all means capture him, try him, hang him for murder, but you'll end up chasing killer dogs all over the moors for the next five years. More if they breed. Give it a year and there won't be sheep left on the entire moor."

"So we need to find the crates and the dog's first." remarked the Lieutenant.

Agnes smiled. Sometimes stating the obvious was better for all concerned.

"But they could be scattered all over the moors!" Andrew said.

"They probably are. But they will be in threes!" Agnes replied. "Think about it!" she added before anyone could say anything. "Three dogs attacked Marmaduke. Three were awake in the ships hold, and three more still in the crates."

Everyone nodded. When she explained it like that there was no arguing. Mind you there never was with Agnes. She didn't like arguments. If things ever looked like they may become heated she would give one of her looks and the protagonist would suddenly find themselves agreeing with every word she said. She found her life ran a lot more smoothly like that.

"Can't you just use that damned dish thing again?" The Commander asked.

Agnes gave her arm a rub. "I don't think it's going to be that easy. I could and he could have placed some sort of protection around them. Just suppose my scrying releases the dogs."

"What about the ones running around out there?" Andrew asked. "How many are released already?"

There was a polite cough from the other end of the table. "I know I may be missing something here, but why is he doing it?"

Everyone turned towards Lieutenant Smalls. He gave an apologetic shrug. "He seems to be going to a lot of trouble but I'm blowed if I can see why."

Agnes sat forward in her chair. The ache in her arm had almost disappeared now. "I've been thinking about that."

They all turned to her.

"And I have no idea!"

The next hour was spent in a free ranging and imaginative discussion as to why someone would go to the lengths of smuggling crates of killer dogs onto the moors. They ranged from someone who hates sheep to..... well the ideas stopped there actually. That was until the Lieutenant looked up at the Agnes.

"I think you said it earlier."

Agnes raised an eyebrow.

The Lieutenant explained. "You said "if they breed". Perhaps that's just what he's doing, perhaps he's breeding them up there."

"Why?" Marmaduke asked.

Andrew lent forward. "You could make good money selling them. Guard dogs, fighting dogs, they'd make a pretty profit." He caught the look in Agnes's eyes and added quick. "Of course I would never trade in anything like that."

The Commander gave another of his famous harrumphs. "Why don't we just round 'em all up, dogs an all. Shoot the dogs and lock the bounder in our dungeon until he talks."

Agnes was about to say something about the type of military thinking that was losing them the American Colonies and that would lead to escalating troubles into wars for the next three hundred years.

"It would be nice to find out why." Agnes said gently. "But perhaps there are better ways of going about things. A more holistic approach."

The Commander grunted. "Don't bring religion into it!" He said.

Something suddenly clicked at the back of Agnes's mind. She looked up at the Commander. "Just say that again?" She asked.

The Commander blinked. "I said don't bring religion into it. I think!" He looked around the table for confirmation. Everyone nodded.

"Gentlemen! I need time. There are things I must do. We will meet here again." She looked across at the Commander and gave him a special look. "One of your rather splendid working breakfasts Commander?"

He agreed. He hadn't really had a choice as Agnes had fixed him with one of her looks.

Before the meeting broke up Agnes made sure they all had tasks to do. Marmaduke was dispatched to make sure everything was fine up at the farmhouse. This time Agnes gave him a charm that would allow him to enter the protection area. She asked Andrew to try to trace the movements of "The Merchant" as far back as possible and to try to ascertain who had hired her. The Lieutenant was asked to prepare a troop of soldiers and keep them in readiness. Finally the Commander was charged with supplying the breakfast.

As they walked downhill towards the Old Town Agnes noticed a black crow hopping along a wall on the opposite side of the road. She flicked out a finger. The crow exploded in a cloud of black feathers.

She turned towards Andrew. "If I were you I'd shoot every crow you see!"

That night he made sure he locked every door and every window. He fell asleep sat in an armchair in front of the fireplace with a pistol on his knee. He had built up the fire to make sure no crow could get down the chimney.

Once they were inside the house Agnes went to the kitchen and returned with an armful of packages. She turned to Marmaduke. "Give these to the Boggles. Tell them there's more, but I need their help. I need them to help you find out where the dogs and crates are hidden."

Marmaduke looked at her with his one good eye. "They won't do it. They are too scared to go on the moor, those dogs eat Boggles!"

Agnes patted the package and handed it to Marmaduke. "Tell them this will protect them, and the fact that you are going with them. One of those potions is for you."

Chapter Eleven

After Marmaduke left Agnes opened her hand and moved it around the room and across the ceiling. The protection was total. No one could enter. No one could even see inside. She went down her cellar and entered the twenty first century.

She went to her kitchen and reacquainted herself with Mr Tetley's finest product. She looked out of the window. The snow was even deeper. It was now making a small drift against her back door. A radio came to life and she listened to a long list of closed schools and blocked roads. Power lines and telephone wires were down all over the place. She flicked a light switch, nothing happened. She looked across the road and saw a candle burning. A power cut! She shook her head. Any minute now there would be an anxious knocking on her door, a concerned neighbour making sure she was alright, asking her if she needed anything. Oh, she knew they meant well. They were concerned and it was good of them. It was especially good of the woman at number 27 who kept turning up at her door with Tupperware containers full of hot soup. No matter how hard Agnes tried she just couldn't warm to the woman, neither did she like her soup.

She had just made sure her curtains were closed and sat down in front of her computer when someone knocked at her door. As she opened it she made sure her visitor saw the large mug of steaming tea in her hand and the warm glow of dozens of scented candles lighting the inside of her house.

The visitor left quickly and waded through the snow back to their own house. As they stumbled along they kicked themselves for not thinking of buying a camping stove and investing in large quantities of scented candles.

Agnes sat back down in front of her computer, waved her hand and the screen sprang to life. Within seconds she was scanning a variety of documents, articles and web sites. The fact that she had no power didn't matter, the computer was never plugged in anyway. Neither did it matter that it wasn't logged onto the internet, especially as her house wasn't equipped with broadband, or any other band for that matter.

Agnes had originally searched for black dogs. That had been a mistake; the screen was full of them. Some of them were fighting dogs, some were hunting dogs and others were wearing a variety of cute clothing. As long as she lived (and that had been very long time indeed!), she could never understand the mentality of people who insisted on dressing up their dogs.

She refined her search. Then she refined it again, and again, and again.

Eventually she found what she was looking for under a search for religious cults and black dogs. She had read a long article until she realised she was reading the reviews and articles about an album entitled "Religious Cults and Demon Dogs" by a Finnish Death Metal band. It sounded interesting so she had to listen, anyway the night was young. She moved her finger and the play button switched to on. Within seconds the blast of noise rattled the doors walls and windows. She turned it down. It was the first time Agnes had ever exposed herself to death metal, Finnish or otherwise. She found it interesting. She was about to turn it off when a lyric caught her attention. She flicked her finger and the song replayed. There it was again, however the singer's voice was layered underneath a screaming guitar. She played it again and this time the lyrics appeared on the screen.

"When devil dogs roam the moors,

And black crows prowl the skies

Red eyes will predict

Beelzebub will rise...."

She blinked. It couldn't be. The lyrics fitted. She looked up the band. It seemed they had been infamous, but had split up some years previously due to the death of the lead singer. She checked out the band's name. It was called Nostaa Demonit, Agnes translated it to read Raise The Demons. Well that was appropriate. She flicked a finger and a picture of the band appeared on the screen. It was of four young men with long hair, dressed in a variety of black leather and metal studs. She picked out the lead singer. His name was Tapio Lillmans. He had a pierced nose and was heavily tattooed. She could make out the usual Celtic patterns. She was about to clear the screen when she notice a cross in the centre of one of the tattoos. It was of a cross. She did a double take. It was an image of Ralphs Cross.

It took her another hour and many e-mails and messages left on various social media sites and chat rooms before she began to get close. The she received and e-mail. It was in Finnish. She translated.

"Why are you interested in Nostaa Demonit?"

She answered that she was a journalist researching Finnish Death Metal and had come across their work. After some time an e-mail came back. It contained a long number and the message "Skype Me."

She had no idea whatsoever Skype was, but she moved her fingers and the Skype logo appeared on the screen, some images moved and flashed and then she was looking at a youngish man with very long black hair.

The two stared at each other before he spoke. The picture was slightly out of sync with the sound and at first Agnes couldn't make out what the young man was saying. She clicked a finger and the image and sound synchronised.

"You are a journalist?" he asked.

Agnes nodded her head and thought quickly. "It's Radio Scarborough, a digital radio station. We've played some of your material."

The man on the screen was quick. "Which track?"

Agnes was quicker. "I can't pronounce the name but the lyrics were about devil dogs and moors."

The young man's face fell and he shook his head slightly. "That was not a good track!"

"It sounded alright to me!" Agnes remarked.

The young man shook his head. "No. It was, how you say, not good, unlucky."

Agnes looked puzzled. "Why was it unlucky?"

The man paused. "Will you broadcast this?"

Agnes gave a non committal look. "It all depends on what you tell me!"

The man nodded "It was the last song that Tapio wrote."

So the singer was also the song writer. "What was the song about? The lyrics seem a bit obscure."

The man turned very serious. He looked off screen and his arm moved out of picture. When it returned he was holding a bottle of beer. He raised it to his lips and took a deep drink.

"Tapio was into the occult. Oh I know we're all meant to be in some death metal cult or other but he went deeper. He found a weird cult concerning devil dogs and some sort of demon. He researched it a lot. When we weren't working he went all over the place. Germany, Romania, Denmark, Norway, he even went to England. Somewhere called Yorkshire North Moors. He took photographs there and even had a tattoo done of the place he visited. It was some ancient stone cross. There was an argument. We told him he shouldn't have a tattoo featuring a Christian symbol. He insisted it had nothing to do with Christianity, it had something to do with the devil dog cult. A day or so later he tuned up with the lyrics. We recorded it and added it onto our last album. It was a good song."

"What happened to Tapio?"

The young man looked away for a second as if remembering times past. "It was just as was reported. We were in the country working in a recording studio. One evening in a break he went for a walk. We never saw him again. They found his body a few days later in the woods. Everyone thinks he got lost and wandered around. They think he must have been attacked by wolves. I never saw the body, but there again, there was very little left of the body to be seen."

The young man fell into a silent reflection. Agnes let him have his moment.

Eventually, out of politeness and to change the subject, she asked what the young man was doing at the present.

He smiled. "I am working with a new band. We are adopting traditional Finnish folk tunes to a death metal genre. It is proving to be very interesting."

Agnes nodded. I bet it is she thought. She smiled and thanked the young man for his co-operation.

He raised his bottle to the screen in a toast. "Before you go I have a question. Why is an elderly lady representing death metal on an English radio station?"

Agnes smiled. "Oh you would be amazed at what us elderly English ladies get up to."

The Finnish musician laughed and the image closed down.

"Well!" thought Agnes, "that went better than I expected. A very nice young man."

Dawn was braking as her printer finally stopped. She waved her hand and the computer closed down. She looked behind her. The kitchen light was blazing away. Sometime in the night the power had returned. She waved her hand and the scented candles melted away.

Chapter Twelve

As Agnes was sitting at her computer a black shape was racing across the countryside and open moorland. The snow had drifted across the tracks and gullies but at least it had stopped falling. Marmaduke's journey was uneventful and he arrived at the farmstead without incident. He approached the farm carefully holding the charm in the palm of his hand. All he felt as he passed through the protective shield was a slight tingle. He entered the farmhouse. Everything was quiet. He heard a noise in the kitchen and looked in to see Joan working with the shepherd's wife preparing food. They looked up as he popped his head around the doorway.

"The men are feeding the sheep. The Boggles are meant to be helping but I'm not sure the sheep appreciate them. I think John might have put them to work in the barn."

Marmaduke walked across the farmyard to the barn. As soon as he entered the building he found himself in a world of chaos. The Boggles had found piles of straw and were running and jumping in it, on it, and throwing it around. Some were climbing up into the roof beams and leaping down. He took one look and let out a growl. The Boggles froze. He clapped his hands and they gathered around him. He looked at the one who he assumed was the leader.

"We need to talk!" He said.

Marmaduke took his arm and led him to the old bench and sat down. The rest of the Boggles gathered behind them.

Marmaduke explained Agnes's plan. At first the Boggle shook his head. Marmaduke reached into his bag and pulled out the packages Agnes had prepared. The Boggles eyes grew wide. There were small individual packages containing tangerines and lots of shiny sparkly things. Now Boggles like nothing better than sparkly shiny things, unless its tangerines. In order to own this treasure the Boggles would have waded through fire. Admittedly it would have to be a small fire but when it comes down to it everything's just a matter of scale. Of course the agreement was made when Marmaduke pulled out the final item. It was a large bag of cloaking powder. He took a pinch and sprinkled it over his legs. The air shimmered slightly and his legs disappeared. The Boggles were watching wide eyed. The leader took a tiny pinch and sprinkled it over himself. He disappeared. The rest of the Boggles scattered.

It took some time to gather all the Boggles back in one place and even more time for them to understand what was being asked of them. At first there was a lot of shaking of heads and wringing of small hands. Then there was a lot of sniffing of tangerines and examining shiny sparkly things. Marmaduke sat back and watched as they discussed the offer. Of course to describe the bickering, arguing and general uproar as a discussion would be to misuse the word discussion. But eventually a sort of order prevailed and one at a time the Boggles agreed to undertake the task. For some the decision had been made easier because they had already eaten their tangerines. It was then that Marmaduke realised the subtlety of Agnes's gifts. After they had sprinkled themselves with the powder and eaten the tangerines they became visible again, but only to each other. The tangerines were a part of the spell.

Once they were all cloaked Marmaduke became aware that his own senses had suddenly increased in power. From inside the barn he could smell the moorland heather and the damp marsh. He could smell water that ran across the moor in small streams. He could hear a far off curlew as if it were stood next to him. He could hear the breeze rustling in the woods and the snow as it dropped off the leaves and branches of distant trees. He led the Boggles out of the barn, through the protective screen and into the surrounding moorland.

Across the snow and the heather he could see the slight yellowish glow of animal tracks. They were the tracks of the three dogs that had followed him into the woods. As he let out a small growl the air around him shimmered and the Boggles watched as a large cat like shape began to form around him. He gave a nod to the head Boggle and bounded off following the tracks away from the woods onto the open moor. There were a number of flurries in the snow. The heather rose and fell as twelve, or was it thirteen Boggles raced across the moor.

One thing that Boggles do really well is run. They are very good at it. When you are only one foot high and live unseen among the world of men, with birds of prey and occasional dogs and foxes to contend with, the one thing you learn from a very early age is to run, and run very fast.

They covered the ground very quickly and were soon following the tracks themselves. As they crested the top of a small hill Marmaduke signalled for the party to stop. The tracks led down to a small valley and an old stone barn. Marmaduke sniffed, something didn't smell right. There was a movement on the roof of the building. Black shapes were hopping around on the snow. Crows, at least four of them. He looked down at the Boggles and pointed towards the birds. There was a scuffle and the snow scattered. Marmaduke watched as the Boggles split up and raced towards the building, invisible to the crows who were still hopping up and down on the roof top. As Marmaduke watched the snow on the roof seemed to spin and flurry. From inside the building Marmaduke heard low growls. The Boggles ran straight back to him. In their hands were the bodies of four dead crows hanging upside down, their feathers and wings torn, their beaks hanging open. Marmaduke noticed their sightless eyes. They were bright red.

He loped across the ground until he reached the barn. He stopped by the door and listened. He could hear a heaving breathing behind the door. He wasn't too sure if it was the sound of a single dog, he couldn't tell. He crept nearer the door and silently examined it, holding his breath as he felt the door frame and the fixings. It wasn't secure. He took a step back and pulled both pistols from his belt. Then leaning back, he kicked the door as hard as he could. It collapsed inwards. There was a loud growl and a black shape leapt out of the darkness of the barn towards him. He fired both guns. The black shape twisted and writhed in the air. Before it hit the floor Marmaduke had dropped his pistol and drawn his sword. He decapitated the creature in mid-air. As it creature fell Marmaduke paused at the door and listened. Everything was silent. He entered cautiously and waited as his eyes adjusted to the darkness. He then noticed six crates stacked up at the far end of the barn. One was open. Within seconds he gathered up some old dry straw, some timbers and what remained of the door. He reached into his pocket and pulled out a small flint. The spark ignited the straw. He blew on it and a flame appeared. He waited until the fire had taken hold and was lapping against the sides of the wooden crates. Satisfied with the result he dragged the headless body of the dead creature across the barn door and threw it towards the fire. Then he ran out and crashed straight into a gaggle of Boggles. He grabbed the ones he'd run over and shouted at the others. They all ran. Behind them the building simply exploded.

The force lifted Marmaduke off his feet and threw him flat on his face. All of a sudden it began to rain bits of stone and slate, and the occasional Boggle. He stood up and turned around. The building had been destroyed. All that remained was a pile of burning rubble. As he brushed himself down he heard a distant howl echo across the moorland. He heard rusting and looked down to see to see the Boggles gathering around his legs. They had survived the explosion, but a number had been caught by the blast. Some appeared to be singed, others had lost chunks of hair, a couple had lost their eyebrows, most of them had lost their hats. Marmaduke felt his jacket being pulled and looked down at the leader. He wasn't looking very happy.

Marmaduke bent down to catch the little mans words.

"Never mention anything about big bang! Boggles don't like blowings up. Makes Boggles very nervous."

Marmaduke tried to keep a straight face. "I'll try to give you more warning next time."

At the words "next time" the Boggles fell to arguing among themselves. There was some pushing and shoving. Marmaduke sighed. Just what he needed. However the Boggles weren't the worse of his problems. The explosion must have been heard all over the moors. Surely the sound had alerted the man in black. He winced as he remembered Agnes's instructions. "Locate them" she had said. What she hadn't mentioned was destroying them. He gave a shrug. Well at least there were fewer dogs to worry about now, and that can't be a bad thing. He tried to remember how many were left and failed. Marmaduke was not very good at mathematics. If he had been he would have calculated that somewhere out on the moors were another thirteen dogs.

He cocked his head and tried to remember which direction the howling had come from. What was left of the building was still burning. In its flickering light Marmaduke saw black dots appearing in the sky. A flock of crows was gathering, making looping swoops over the remains and the rubble. He signalled for the Boggles to lay on the ground. He wasn't taking any chances with the invisibility thing, and squatted down himself. It seemed as if the crows were examining the damage below them. It dawned on him, of course they would. They were the man in black's eyes and ears. As quickly as they arrived the crows rose up in the air. They circled the site a couple of times and then split up into smaller groups and flew off in separate directions. One group flew over Marmaduke. He decided to follow them. He rose and signalled for the Boggles to follow him.

They ran across the moor, leaping over small streams and sheep tracks. Ahead the crows rose in the air and formed another circle. Again they repeated their pattern of rising and falling. This time they were over a small outcrop of rock marked by two sparse trees desperately clinging onto the surface. After a lot of swooping the little flock rose in the air and flew off. Marmaduke noted the direction before walking up to the outcrop.

It was a little while before he found the small cave burrowed under the centre of the outcrop. He bent down and wriggled. He attuned his vision and saw three crates positioned towards the back of the cave. He remembered Agnes's words. "Locate!" He looked down. The Boggles were peering into the cave. A couple of the more braver ones actually ventured inside, but soon came out again when they saw the boxes. Marmaduke had an idea, he looked up at the outcrop. Some of it didn't look very stable. He ran around it and stood on its surface. From the top he had a good view of the surrounding moorland. He looked down. The rocks beneath his feet wouldn't take much moving. He signalled to the Boggles and within seconds they were on their knees scrabbling at the earth with their hands, pulling out grass and earth. Soon they had destabilised the ground on top of the outcrop. Marmaduke nodded and drew his sword, forcing it between the rocks. Using the blade as a lever he loosened to rock until it began to rock. He looked down and signalled to the Boggles. They began pushing and scrabbling, the rock moved, paused and then fell taking earth and loose rocks with it. It fell down the face of the rock. Encouraged, the Boggles continued kicking and pushing the earth and the stones down the outcrop.

Marmaduke left them to it and returned to the bottom of the rockface. As he hoped the entrance to the cave was completely blocked. He moved back a couple of steps as another shower of rock and earth bounced down and rolled to a halt in front of him. He gave a wave and in seconds he was surrounded by the Boggles inspecting the result of their work. Some of them ran up and down the pile. Other jumped up and down forcing the debris deeper into the small cave.

"That sorts that!" Marmaduke thought.

He led his small party back up onto the moor.

"Now what?" he asked himself.

He looked at the sky. There was no sign of the crows. He figured they must have checked the other locations, found the crates unharmed and returned to their master.

He estimated the distance they had travelled and tried hard to remember the map. He wasn't sure where he was and the snow didn't make things any easier. Without knowing why he decided to head off south. It was as good a direction as any other, and it was on the way back to the farmstead and beyond that Scarborough. The air shimmered and an invisible giant black cat ran across the open moorland followed by twelve or thirteen invisible Boggles who, despite having been blow up, singed, and having dirt under their finger nails, were actually beginning to enjoy themselves. There were still dogs out there but Marmaduke didn't know where. As he ran he sniffed the air. Apart from snow nothing entered his nostrils. He made for the farmstead again.

As they entered the protective area their invisibility wore off. Outside the farmhouse they found Whitby John on guard with a gun across his legs. He was asleep and Marmaduke had great difficulty in stopping the Boggles from climbing all over him and waking him up. They entered the house as quietly as a hoard of Boggles could, which wasn't very quiet at all. Soon Marmaduke could hear the farmer's wife moving around above them.

The door opened and Whitby John stood there.

"I only shut my eyes for a moment!" he aid

Marmaduke shrugged. On seeing Whitby John awake the Boggles jumped up and down and insisted on telling him of their adventures and bravery. It would have made sense if the twelve, or thirteen, hadn't all spoken at once. As they tried to shout over each other some began pushing and shoving the others. A fight would have soon broken out if Joan hadn't have appeared at the doorway holding a very large heather broom. She lifted it up and began to wave it around. Everyone in the room fell silent.

"Bed!" she said.

Everyone scrabbled for a sleeping space. Marmaduke smiled as he let himself out of the house. One more run around the moor and then back to the Scarborough Garrison for a decent breakfast. As the black cat like shape crossed the protective barrier and disappeared over a small hill he hoped there would be kedgeree.

After a while he found himself on the top of the moor. The snow had stopped falling and a white blanket stretched out below him disguising walls and blurring the landscape. A thin light was filtering over the horizon, dawn wasn't far away. In the distance a shape appeared silhouetted against the skyline. Marmaduke recognised it. It was Ralphs Cross. He veered off towards it hoping to trace the road that led off the moor. As he approached he saw a tiny flicker of light at its base.

He stopped and dropped onto all fours. Slowly he crept across the moor until he could see the shape of the man holding the lantern. He flattened himself into the snow and crawled nearer. The man seemed to be on his knees at the foot of the stone cross. His arms were moving as if he were placing something around the bottom of it, on the raised stone plinth. As he looked the man raised his head and looked directly at him, his eyes were bright red. Despite laying in the snow Marmaduke knew the man had seen him. The man said something and Marmaduke became aware of a second figure. This one held a gun pointing straight at him. He saw the flash of the exploding powder and rolled to one side. The ball thudded into the moor where he been laying.

He rose to his feet and drew out his own pistol.
Before he could raise it the man in black with the
reds eyes seemed to vanish and melt away. In his
place was a large black dog. The biggest dog
Marmaduke had ever seen. Its eyes burned bright
red and its mouth slobbered open showing huge
fangs. It leapt and bounded across the moor,

quickly eating up the distance between them.
Marmaduke fired. The ball hit its target. He knew it
did. It just didn't have any effect. The beast was
almost on him when Marmaduke moved. There was
a blur and a large cat shape leapt to one side as the
beasts jaws snapped at the air where Marmaduke
had been standing. He could smell the fetid breath
as it twisted in the air trying for a second bite. The
air blurred once more and Marmaduke stood there.
In the space of two seconds he had thrown two of
his knives. The first bounced off the creatures hide.
The second glanced the front of the beasts head
nicking the corner of its eye, before bouncing off to
join the first knife among the snow and heather. The
creature stopped, raised its head and howled.

Marmaduke's spine turned to ice as he heard the howl answered. The replies broke out in all directions. The dogs were loose. The creature in front of him snorted and pulled its lips back to show its fangs.

Marmaduke knew he was in trouble. Two or three dogs and a loaded weapon was a fair fight. Goodness knows how many dogs and a wounded giant dog and no guns were odds he didn't like. The howling was getting nearer. If he was to make a move it had to be now, otherwise the dogs would be on him. The air shimmered and a giant black cat leapt over the howling dog.

The move was so sudden that the creature didn't have time to react. As the black cat passed overhead it raked a talon down the back of the giant dog. The creature let out another howl. It turned and once again snapped at thin air. The cat shape had gone. The creature growled as it spotted the cat shape cross a nearby hill crest. It let out another howl and thirteen black dogs ran across the moor and settled in a circle around it. The air shimmered and the man in black with the red eyes appeared in the middle of the circle of dogs. One off his eyes was bleeding from the corner, the back of his long coat was ripped and torn. He wiped away a trickle of blood with the back of his hand and turned and strode back to the stone cross. The second man held the lantern and the man in black returned to task he was doing before he was disturbed.

Chapter Thirteen

Breakfast in the Garrison Commanders office was always a splendid affair. The Commander firmly believed that an army marched on its stomach and that the best and most important meal of the day was breakfast. The table was bending under the weight of platters of fried bacon, ham, chops of pork and lamb, eggs (poached, scrambled and fried), sausages, kedgeree, with freshly made bread and pots of freshly brewed coffee and tea.

The Commander was especially pleased with the tea. For years he had had to put up with badly brewed tea. It was the best quality, he knew because he ordered it himself, but it seemed to him that the army had a special way of spoiling its delicate flavour so it ended up tasting like metal polish mixed with old gunpowder. In fact its enhanced flavour was nothing to do with the army cooks. It had to do with Andrew Marks currently tucking into a lamb chop. After tasting the tea himself he had sought out the supplier and simply asked him to stop substituting the expensive and fine blended tea the Commander ordered for the cheap and inferior type that could only be described as sweepings from the factory floor. At first the supplier objected. He was making a good profit on his enterprise. Then Andrew explained that the supplier just might run into some problems if he ever wished to import and export goods out of the harbour. As the supplier used the harbour everyday of his commercial life he quickly rethought his original position. A trader does that when faced with the choice of losing a little or losing the lot.

Across the table Lieutenant Smalls was watching Agnes as she placed strips of bacon between two halves of a bread bun. The more he looked the more he thought the idea might catch on. Just as she took her first bite the door opened and in walked Marmaduke. For a second everyone stopped eating and looked up at him. He was panting and, compared to his normal state looked decidedly worn. Agnes noticed that knives were missing from his bandoleer.

"Tough night?" she asked

He nodded as he pulled up a chair and helped himself to a plate full of kedgeree. Agnes noticed he didn't bother using a knife or fork.

Andrew coughed. "Whilst Marmaduke is breaking his fast I have some information you might like to hear."

He had their attention and pulled out a paper and began reading from it.

"The Merchant is registered in Newcastle. Usually it travels up and down the coast with whatever cargo it can get. However some time ago now it made a trip across the North Sea. It turned up in Antwerp. We lose track of it for a couple of months and then it turns up in Hartlepool. From there it returns to Antwerp and then returns to Whitby. Then it sails from Whitby down here."

"Did you find out what it was carrying?" Agnes asked.

Andrew drew out a second piece of paper out of his pocket. "I did. According to the manifest, when it left Antwerp the first time, it was carrying ten large crates of samples off earth."

Everyone looked up from whatever it was they were eating. Andrew checked the paper. "It was also carrying ten kegs of Geneva gin and some tobacco." He placed a finger on a line of figures. "Although when they arrived in Hartlepool they only declared eight kegs of gin."

"Why crates of earth?" Asked the Lieutenant.

"I have no idea whatsoever, but they carried a similar cargo back from Antwerp on their second trip. Another ten crates of earth samples."

Agnes mused aloud. "The Captain said he had shipped twenty five crates in all. He didn't say where he'd shipped them from. So they originated on the continent and were dropped up and down the coast."

The Lieutenant interrupted her. "So where did the other five crates come from?"

Now it was his turn to be stared at.

The Commander stopped demolishing his lamb chop long enough to splutter. "Bounders are breeding!" He gave a grunt and went back to ripping the meat from the bone with his teeth.

Agnes looked across the table at him "You're right Commander!"

The comment caused the Commander to stop eating. "Right? About what?"

Agnes took a sip of her tea. Despite the it being the special blend the Commander ordered it was nowhere near as good as that produced by Mr Tetley. "That's precisely what our man in black is doing. He is breeding, growing those dogs."

Now it was her turn to be stared at.

It was the Commander who asked the obvious question. "Why?"

Agnes put her tea down and slid the cup away from her. She reached for the coffee pot. "He needs a certain number of them to conduct some sort of quasi religious ceremony." She said.

Even Marmaduke stopped eating when he heard that.

Agnes sat back in her chair. "Last night......" she began and continued to tell of her research into religious cults and black dogs. Of course she never mentioned her computer, or Skype, or Finnish Death Metal. She did mention that the cult somehow used the black dogs to help them raise a demon.

At the mention of the word demon the Commander spat his tea across the table and the Lieutenant crossed himself.

Marmaduke looked up from his platter. "Last night the man in black and his assistant were doing something up at Ralphs Cross, seemed to me they were making some sort of preparations."

Agnes demanded more information and, after licking his fingers clean Marmaduke told them about his night on the moors. When he finished there was a silence around the table broken only by the Commander murmuring the word "Boggles" over and over again and shaking his head.

Agnes looked at Marmaduke. "You blew six dogs up?"

Marmaduke nodded. "If, as we seem to be assuming, that the dogs are in the crates, yes. Only I didn't blow them up. They blew themselves up."

"Only because you set fire to them!" Andrew remarked.

Agnes thought for a few minutes whilst everyone else tried to digest this new information.

"The stuff in the crates can't just be earth. The crates must contain some sort of alchemy that preserves the dogs and keeps them alive." she finally said.

Andrew gave a little snort. "You mean they go in as puppies and come out as giant killer dogs?"

"I'm not too sure that puppies come into it!" She said. "I think that with some sort of power, some sort of magic if you like, our man in black with the red eyes can create these beasts. He brought some with him and grew the other five here."

"What's Ralphs Cross got to do with things?" Andrew asked.

"That's where he's planning on raising his demon, and, if Marmaduke is right, I would hazard a guess that he is planning on doing it tonight."

"If he needs twenty five dogs he's got problems. Half of them are dead. Marmaduke observed.

Agnes shook her head. "Perhaps he doesn't need that many. Perhaps the rest of the dogs are in a pack that will be controlled by the demon!"

The Commander gave another grunt. "You mean to tell me we are about to have a demon stalking across the moors with a pack of giant dogs?" he paused and looked around the table. "Am I the only one thinking that not only is it far-fetched but bordering on the insane?"

Agnes nodded. "Oh our man in black with the red eyes is insane. He lives only for this ceremony. He has tried before, and ...." She added enigmatically, "he will no doubt try again."

She looked towards the Lieutenant. "Are your men ready to march?"

He looked straight back at her. "We can have a mounted troop up there inside three hours."

Agnes nodded. "Do it. I would like a ring of steel around Ralphs Cross. Tell them to form a circle about a hundred yards from it. Make sure they are well hidden, oh and make sure that en-route you shoot every crow you see."

She looked across to Marmaduke. "Back to the farm I'm afraid. Gather up those Boggles and see what you can do to hinder the man, but be careful. You've had one lucky escape. Anyway you'll have an advantage this time. I'm coming with you."

She stroked her mending arm. "This is personal!" she added.

The Commander always one for military action insisted on accompanying his troops. No one could dissuade him, after all he was in charge. Anyway Agnes thought, he needed some action and it made a nice change to find a military commander willing to join his troops in the field.

The plans were made and it was time for action.

Before they left for the moors Agnes popped into the Three Mariners. Baccy Lad was behind the bar, hard at work polishing anything that could be polished. She noticed that there were curtains fixed onto the inside of the windows, which in turn were sparkling. Agnes could never remember having ever been able to see through them before, and she had drunk in there for many years. Now the interior of the bar was light and breezy. The far end was decorated by a large copper vase filled with some freshly cut flowers. She looked out at the thin layer of snow in the street and wondered where the widow had got them from. She could hear the clatter and noise coming from the kitchen at the rear of the bar. As she opened the door a cloud of steam drifted past her. Inside Mrs Pateley was washing every remaining tankard and every plate and dish and platter she could find. Agnes didn't disturb her but shut the door quietly behind her.

"I suppose you had a hand in all this!"

Agnes looked across the bar room to the fireplace where Salmon Martin sat with Martin Tong. They had cloths in their hands and were polishing small glasses until they sparkled.

"The place will never be the same again!" Bemoaned Martin

"Good!" Said Agnes as she left the building and closed the door behind her.

Chapter Fourteen

By the time the troops had gathered in the Castle courtyard Agnes and Marmaduke were already on their way. Marmaduke wasn't too sure how they arrived at the farmhouse so quickly. All he knew was that Agnes kept moving her fingers and the countryside seemed to flash past him.

When they arrived the snow was melting and the area around the farmhouse was full of slush and mud. The sheep in the pen skittered nervously as Marmaduke passed by. Agnes flicked out a finger and they settled down again.

"I wish I could do that!" A voice remarked.

They turned around to see the shepherd walking across to them. His dogs were walking quietly around his feet. He doffed his cap as he stopped in front of Agnes.

"I don't think I ever got round to thanking you properly." He nodded towards the sheep. "Brought 'em all in safely. It's a good shepherd that brings 'em all home."

He turned round and walked back to his cottage. Agnes realised she'd just been paid the highest of compliments. She allowed herself a little smile.

As they entered the farmhouse the Boggles made a dash for Agnes. They jumped up at her and danced around her skirts. She looked down at them. She could recognise flattery when she saw it. She put her hand in her pocket and pulled out a small round shiny object. The Boggles fell quiet, their eyes fixed on the sparkly thing. She passed it to the nearest Boggle who held it carefully in his hands as if it were the most precious thing in the world. She repeated the action another thirteen times until each Boggle sat quietly holding a shiny sparkly thing in their own hands, turning it over and over again, their eyes wide with wonder.

Whitby John rose to his feet and offered her the chair nearest to the fire. She graciously declined it and walked through to the kitchen. Joan was busy scrubbing her table surface. By a quick glance Agnes could tell that he woman had cleaned and polished and scrubbed everything that could be cleaned, polished and scrubbed. Agnes walked across to her and gently placed a hand on her shoulder.

"It will be over tonight. Tomorrow we will be able to bury him and lay him to rest."

The woman let out a deep sob. Agnes put her arm around her and allowed the woman the opportunity to weep, her sobs shaking her body. Agnes held her tight until the sobs stopped and the woman took a step back. She wiped away her tears with the sleeve of her dress. Agnes flicked a finger and the kettle behind them boiled, which was odd as it wasn't on the stove. Agnes herself carried the tray into the living room. Whitby John took a cup and looked up at Agnes.

"I don't suppose you had a chance to look into the Three Mariners?"

Agnes nodded. "I was there this morning. It's still standing."

Whitby John wasn't comforted. "They'll all be drinking at The Beehive now." he said and shook his head sadly as he blew on his tea.

"I think you might be pleasantly surprised!" Agnes said as she drained her cup and replaced it on the tray. "Now we have business to attend to. John, you stay here. Make sure your guns are loaded. I'm pretty certain the shield will hold, but if anything, and I mean anything that isn't me or Marmaduke or a Boggle appears, shoot first and don't bother with any questions."

She looked across to Marmaduke. "Go get the shepherd and his family across here."

She looked towards Joan. "I'm afraid everyone must stay under your roof tonight. The good news is that the Boggles will be coming with us."

The farmer's widow smiled for the first time in days.

As Marmaduke collected the shepherds family Agnes called the Boggles around her and explained at great length and in great detail what she required of them. As she explained there was a great deal of shaking of heads and the wringing of hands. She spoke some more, this time in a hushed whisper. As she spoke the Boggles eyes grew wider and wider. Then they all began to nod. When Marmaduke arrived back with the shepherd and his family Agnes had her own little army.

As they left the farmhouse and crossed the yard Agnes turned and moved her hands in a circular motion. For a brief moment the farmhouse shimmered. Then it vanished. In its place was the shepherd's cottage. Marmaduke turned around. The farm house was standing where the cottage stood. The air shimmered once more. He looked at Agnes she shrugged.

"Just a bit of confusion. It's all done with mirrors."

Marmaduke scratched behind his ear. "But you've just swopped them around. Anyone can tell that's the farmhouse. It looks like the farmhouse."

Agnes gave him one of her infuriating enigmatic looks. "It might look like the farmhouse. That's the trick!"

Marmaduke shook his head. Sometimes it was better not to ask.

They left the protective shield and walked up onto the open moor. The first thing they heard was the howling, and then the fluttering. From nowhere a flock of crows appeared in the sky. Fearing the worse Agnes moved her hands and arms in a circling motion. The snow around them blurred. Where thirteen Boggles had been standing the air was full of flapping and fluttering and thirteen peregrine falcons suddenly shot into the sky. Marmaduke looked up. There were fourteen of them, Agnes had joined in.

The peregrines hit the flock of crows in the same way a bowling ball hits the pins when a strike has been scored. There were puffs and explosions of black feathers dropped out of the sky. As he watched the sky above him Marmaduke suddenly froze. Behind him he could hear the sound of heavy, wet breathing. Without pausing to turn around he leapt backwards through the air. He passed the creature mid-air as it leapt into the space where he had been standing. The creature bit the air and turned to find its prey. As he landed Marmaduke pulled out his pistol and fired. The ball hit the creature right between the eyes forming a third and very bloody third eye. The creature yowled and fell over dead.

"I'd go and retrieve your ball." A voice behind him said.

He turned to see Agnes standing behind him.

"Why would I be doing that?" he asked.

"Because it's silver. They all are!"

Marmaduke looked into his pouch. All his pistol balls shone. He was about to say something when the air around him was filled with whooping and fluttering and arms and legs. Thirteen Boggles lay spread in disarray among the snow and heather. He watched as they scrambled to their feet.

"Nippy little creatures in the air. Haven't worked out how to land properly though." Agnes observed.

"Where now?" Marmaduke asked her.

"Well we have lost any element of surprise. He must have found us as soon as we left the protective screen. This isn't going as planned. We were meant to be hunting him. Now he's hunting us, and whilst he's got us busy he can concentrate on doing what he came to do."

Marmaduke wasn't sure what she meant, but he reloaded his pistol and checked his bandoleer. He grinned and his fangs appeared over his bottom lip. He was ready.

Agnes moved her head. "Ralph's Cross is over there."

They set off across the moor but hadn't gone half a mile before another flock of crows appeared in the sky. Agnes looked up. The flock was flying well apart, leaving a lot of space between each bird. So, the man in black had seen the falcon attack and learnt. She knew she couldn't repeat the same trick as the fourteen falcons could only attack one crow at a time, and there were dozens of crows. They were circling, preparing to attack. She moved her hand and a protective shield opened up above them like an umbrella. Some of the crows were too close to stop or divert and they crashed into it with a series of splats and showers of blood and black feathers. The others veered off to glide and swoop above them. The Boggles gathered around Agnes's skirts looking up in apprehension of the black shapes that hung in the sky above them. One crow tried to fly under the umbrella. It landed at Agnes's feet with a knife through its body. Agnes moved her fingers and the protective screen spread down to the floor. She gritted her teeth. The man in black had them pinned down and time was passing. She formed her hands into fists and held them together knuckle to knuckle. The grey sky lit up as bolts of lightning flashed and raked across the sky. It was followed by a second and a third. Singed and burnt black shapes began falling out of the sky marking the unbroken snow.

Agnes moved her hands once more. A vicious hail storm burst overhead. The stones were as big as golf balls. When it stopped just as suddenly as it started there wasn't a crow left in the sky.

She shooed the Boggles away from her skirts and looked at Marmaduke. "Ralph's Cross!"

He nodded and the air blurred around them.

They stopped in a small depression half a mile away from the cross itself. At the bottom of the depression was a puddle covered with a thin layer of ice. Agnes moved her hands and the sky above the depression shimmered.

"Protection. Camouflage, it's just a trick." She said as she reached into her pocket and retrieved some herbs and spices. She broke the ice and sprinkled them over the puddle.

"Let's see what he's up to." She said as she peered into the water.

An image of the stone cross appeared. It didn't look its normal self. Around its base were a number of large black bowls each on holding a dish of red flame. The cross itself had been painted with a number of runes and strange markings. Around the stone cross was a ring of giant black dogs, seated on the moor their giant paws stretched forward, all looking at the cross. There was a protective screen around the whole. Outside of the screen a number of dogs were patrolling the perimeter, sniffing the air and softly growling. In the middle of all this, standing in front of the cross, stood the man in black with the red eyes. Behind him his assistant was unloading the carcass of a dead sheep. He carried it and carefully placed it on the stone plinth on which the cross stood. As he stepped back the dogs raised their heads and howled. The sound made ones blood turn to ice. The man in black with the red eyes took a knife from inside his jacket. It was long and curved and looked very ancient with markings along its blade. He plunged it into the carcass. Blood and innards spilled out over the stone. The flames in the bowls suddenly flared higher and the dogs let out another, louder howl.

Agnes realise the ceremony had started. She moved her hands and the vision in the puddle disappeared. She moved them again and a vision of a troop of soldiers appeared. Agnes shook her head. They were still some way away. She estimated it would take them a further half hour at the very least before they were in position. Although she had no idea how long the ceremony would take to complete she had a nasty feeling the soldiers would arrive too late. A delay was called for. She moved her hand and the vision disappeared. She stood up. The Boggles had all gathered around the puddle and had seen the situation for themselves. They might have been small but they weren't unintelligent. They knew full well the situation they found themselves in. Before they could begin to talk and squabble among themselves Agnes raised her hand for silence. They saw the look on her face and fell quiet, although a few sharp elbows found themselves in a few unprotected ribs. She bent down and whispered a few words. There was much shaking of heads and shuffling of feet. She reached into her pocket and pulled out thirteen bright shiny things. The shaking of heads quickly turned to a frantic sea of nodding heads. Some even jumped up and down in their new found enthusiasm.

Once she had explained her plan and after much pointing and talking among themselves, the Boggles set off. Once they had scrabbled to the top of the depression they ran in all directions hither and thither across the moor, shouting and yelling as they went.

The dogs outside the perimeter raised their heads. They sniffed the air and cocked their ears. Something was on the moor, but despite smelling and hearing something they couldn't see anything. For a few minutes the moor was filled with dogs running in all directions, snarling and snapping. Their jaws slavering as their heads moved from side to side, howling as they ran.

One dog ran straight towards Marmaduke. He drew his sword and, as the dog opened its jaws to rip him apart, Marmaduke side stepped and made a huge sweep with his blade. He cut the dog deeply and it howled and limped away into the heather to lay bleeding, snarling and growling. The noise of the dog attracted the attention of the man in black who looked up from his ministrations. With a look of contempt he flicked a finger. There was a short high pitched scream and a flurry of snow. Agnes looked as a Boggle landed on the moor next to her. Its body was bent in an awkward, twisted shape. She knew it would not be getting to its feet ever again. She looked across the moor and pointed her hand. A bolt of blue lightening flashed across the moor. It exploded and shattered across the man's protective screen. The man in black laughed and Agnes heard a second short high pitched scream.

Meanwhile Marmaduke had undergone a transformation. Now the attacking dogs found themselves faced by a very large black cat that seemed to be equipped with more talons and fangs than any creature they had ever encountered. They were confused. As three dogs edged towards it the ct suddenly leapt into the air and made what could only be described as a kung fu move. As it twisted in the air its claws hung down and raked great bloody gouges into one of the dog's backs. The dog twisted its head so violently that it fell onto its side and lay panting on the heather. The other two dogs watched waiting for an opportunity to attack. Marmaduke was ready. As they sprang the cat like creature seemed to morph into a man whirling a sword and a long dagger. It was too late. As they flew through the air Marmaduke spun and the whirling blades dug deep into the flanks of both dogs. They yowled and landed on the moor thrashing their limbs as blood stained the surrounding snow. They died with their jaws still snapping and foaming.

There was a bright flash in front of him. Marmaduke paused as he tried to clear his sight. He blinked. When his sight returned he saw Agnes holding her hand out, fingers twitching, sending out small bolts of lightning. As they flew through the air they made contact with something and exploded short of their target. Marmaduke glanced across the moor towards the cross. The man in black was standing by the side of the cross holding his arm out in their direction. Marmaduke ducked and rolled across the ground. The earth where he had been standing exploded in a shower of soil and stone. He made a dive for the depression. Meanwhile the remaining dogs and Boggles were still engaged in their deadly game of chase me.

Agnes joined him in the depression. Her hair was singed and her face was blackened.

"Can't get through his shield!" She muttered.

Marmaduke said nothing but looked up as a flurry of snow rolled down the bank at him. It was followed by two large dogs. There were two flashes. The first emanated from Agnes's finger tip and hit one of the dogs full in the chest. The force lifted off its feet and it fell over backwards and lay still on the edge of the ridge.

The second flash had been the glint of the blade of the throwing knife that now lay firmly embedded in the eye of the second dog. It fell dead where it had stood.

Agnes looked across to Marmaduke. "This isn't going well!" She said.

"Seems simple enough to me. Get the man in black!" he replied.

"Not simple. I can't get through his protective shield. It's impenetrable, at least to my powers."

As she said the words a streak of red light flashed over their heads.

"He doesn't seem to have the same problem." Marmaduke observed.

Agnes said nothing. She was thinking. From nowhere the lyrics of a song came to mind.

"When devil dogs roam the moors

Red eyes prowl the skies

The devil dogs are just a sign

Beelzebub will rise."

She ran the words through her head once more, just to make sure she had them in the right order. Then, without warning she leapt onto the rim of the depression and shouted the words into the air, moving her hands and fingers as she shouted.

"When devil dogs roam the moors

Red eyes prowl the skies

The devil dogs are just a sign

Beelzebub will rise."

At first Marmaduke looked at her as if she had gone mad. Then he noticed something moving in the air. As the words came out of her mouth they seemed to appear in front of her. As her fingers moved they formed themselves into a shape that glowed and effervesced, then they formed into a ball and shot across the moorland like a comet leaving a trail behind it.

It hit the man in black's protective shield with spectacular results. It exploded in a sheet of silver flame. Such was the heat it generated that the snow melted for a hundred yards around. Inside the now unprotected area the man in black and his assistant were both blown off their feet by the explosion and lay on their backs. The dogs inside the area began howling. They stood up and, as one, turned and looked towards the place where Agnes stood. On the moor the remaining dogs stopped chasing invisible Boggles and stood sniffing the air. They too joined in with the howling. Agnes moved her arms and the air shimmered once again as she built a protective screen around herself, Marmaduke and the Boggles who had returned to hide under and around her skirts.

Across the moor the man in black and his assistant had regained their feet. The assistant had run to the cart and was climbing into the driving seat. The man in black raised his arms and Agnes's protective shield melted away.

Aware that their prey was now exposed the black dogs came together as a pack. They let out another howl and began to lope slowly across the moor.

Agnes hurriedly made more signs and cast more spells. Each time her arms were raised and her spell cast the man in black raised his arms and her spell dissolved around her. Marmaduke noticed her face was set in a grimace. She frowned as she raised her levels of concentration. She moved her arms again. The man in black mirrored her movements. It would have been a stalemate if it hadn't been for the dogs. They were getting close and closer. Marmaduke could see the flaring of their nostrils and their red maws drooling and slobbering. He checked the remainder of his knives and pointed his pistol at the lead dog.

They were less than a hundred yards away when they raised their heads, gave out one long blood curdling howl and raced towards them. Their speed was so great that Marmaduke was almost caught unawares. He fired his pistol. The shot was hurried and flew harmlessly over the lead dogs head. He had no time to reload and threw his pistol to the ground. He drew his sword and braced himself for the dogs attack. They were so close that he could smell the fetid breath coming from their open mouths. He made ready to swing when a small thunderclap echoed across the moor. Some of the dogs stopped in their tracks and their bodies jumped and twisted in the air. A second thunderclap exploded and the remained of the dogs fell where they stood. He looked across the moor. Two clouds of smoke were rising into the air at the far side. He blinked and made out the bright red of military uniform. The army had arrived. That was confirmed as the voice of the Garrison Commander echoed across the moor shouting a succession of orders. Marmaduke let out a deep breath that he was unaware he had been holding in and looked towards Agnes. She was standing staring at Ralphs Cross. Around her the Boggles were jumping up and down with glee and delight. As usual they crashed into each other, fell over, tumbled over the moor before jumping up again. He ignored their antics and looked across to where Agnes was staring. All he could see was the ancient stone cross, the man in black, and his assistant had completely vanished. He bounded across the moor leaping over the bodies of the dead dogs until he reached the cross. There was no clue as to where the man, his assistant and the cart could have gone. He examined the ground. There were tracks where the cart had stood. Then there were no tracks. He sniffed the air. Nothing, simply no trace. He looked back across the moor. The Boggles had also disappeared. Agnes was walking towards the Commander.

As they met the Commander gave her a salute and harrumphed. "Got here just in time. Dashed near run thing. Almost didn't make it. Don't really know where the last couple of miles went. Seemed to flash by!"

Agnes gave a secret smile. Not all of her gestures and spells had been aimed at the man in black. She looked across the moor to Marmaduke and saw him shake his head. It was a gesture that told her the man in black had escaped. She looked across the moor to where the bodies of the dead dogs lay, their blood seeping into and staining the snow and heather. A movement caught her eye. For a moment she wondered whether one of the creatures was still alive. Then she realised what the movement was. The bodies were dissolving. As she watched they seemed to soak into the surface of the snowy moor. She narrowed her lips. They were returning to the soil. A penny dropped. She turned to the Commander.

"I know it's a great inconvenience, but I have a request. I would like the earth dug up underneath where the dogs are laying."

The Commander blinked. She reiterated her request.

"There's a farmstead along the way. They have a wagon and tools. I'll take some of your men with me. They can bring what they need back here."

She walked to where the dogs had been and paced out an area of some square yards. She looked back at the Commander.

"I have another favour to ask. Once your men have finished here, please bring the earth to me at the farm and then I would be grateful if your troops could help to transport the body of a good man to his funeral and burial at the local church. I'm sure the widow, and the vicar, would appreciate a full congregation. But first I need a close look at that stone cross!"

Agnes marched across the moor until she reached the cross. There was no sign of anything surviving from the unholy ceremony. Everything around the cross had been burned. The receptacles that held the flames were lying in the heather, bent and twisted bits of blackened metal. She examined the cross itself. It had returned to its natural stone state. No trace remained of the markings and symbols. She shook her head. Whoever the man in black was he certainly held a deal of power. Possibly more powerful than herself. She tutted.

"Only tricks!" she said to herself.

She walked across the moor to where the troops were waiting for her.

Across the yard the shepherd was already attending to his sheep. He looked up as Agnes came into the farmyard. She shook her head at the unasked question. It would be better to leave them where they were, for the time being.

Inside the farmhouse everything seemed normal. Whitby John was in the kitchen whilst Joan was dusting, arranging and rearranging the small ornaments on the mantelshelf. The calm was soon shattered as nine, or was it ten Boggles burst in through the back door. On seeing Whitby John they jumped and leapt and shouted, all trying to tell their stories at the same time. Agnes clapped her hands and the little men all fell silent. She made them all sit on the floor and remain still whilst she counted them. There were three missing. She looked at the leader. He gave a slight sad shrug.

"We lost Iggy, Wiggy, and Mortal." He said in a downcast voice. She tried to hide her surprise. She never realised that the Boggles had names. For some reason she never saw them as individuals. Just a number of over enthusiastic little men. She quickly realised she would have to revise her opinion of them.

She squatted down to talk face to face with them. She knew her back would soon be objecting but the little men deserved her respect. They had died helping her.

"Where are their bodies?" She asked softly

The leader indicated the back door. "We bring them here. Off the moor." And then added in a low voice only Agnes could hear. "At least what we could find of them. We only found Iggy's boots."

She shook her head sadly and began to stand. Then thought better of it. She leant forward.

"Could you do me the honour of telling me your names?" she asked.

The Boggle turned and, one at a time, pointed out the eight remaining Boggles.

"Piggy, Ziggy, Figgy, Giddy, Brian, Eli, Jesse, and Richard."

As each of the Boggles were introduced they made a point of standing up and nodding towards Agnes. She acknowledged each one. After he had introduced them she looked at him and raised an eyebrow. He took the hint.

"I am Oggle Boggle!" he said with all seriousness.

Agnes wondered whether he had made the name up just to amuse humans. Then she remembered his three dead companions outside. He probably wasn't. She stood upright and rubbed the small of her back as Whitby John stepped forward.

"I took the liberty of making a coffin. Nowt fancy like. Found some timber and old planking. Figured if there was to be a funeral we'd probably be needing one. I can easily make up another three little ones. Got enough wood left over."

Agnes smiled at him and placed a hand on his shoulder. "You're a good man Whitby John. I thank you. I think that would be a very kind thing to do."

Whitby John nodded and made his way towards the back door. The Boggles jumped up.

"We help, we help!"

Whitby John turned back to look into the room with an expression of what could be only be described as panic. He looked at Agnes and shook his head. She decided his panic deserved a little white lie. She looked down on Oggle Boggle.

"I'm sorry but it is extremely bad luck to make coffins for your fallen comrades. Your duty is to show due reverence, especially during the funeral service tomorrow."

Dawn had broken when a strange procession walked across the moor and joined the road leading to the church. It was so strange that when the vicar opened the church doors he was forced to take a backwards step, not sure of what he was seeing.

In front of him was the elderly lady who had arranged the funeral, that was expected. What wasn't expected was the grieving widow to be supported by an army commander and someone to all appearances seemed to be a highwayman. He was even more surprised to see a full army platoon standing to attention by the side of a wagon. He also noticed that the wagon contained not one but four coffins, one large and three smaller ones that could only be the coffins of children. Before he could say anything the elderly woman took him by his arm and led him back into his small church.

The elderly lady looked into his face. Her eyes seemed to burn into him.

"We need to talk! She said.

Afterwards, later that morning the vicar tried to remember what exactly had occurred during the previous hour. He knew his church had never been so full. He remembered a man who introduced himself as Whitby something or other making a heartfelt and sincere eulogy. Then everything seemed to turn a bit hazy. At the back of his mind was the echo of tiny feet. Of high pitched voices. His final memory was of a platoon of soldiers singing a hymn at the top of their voices under the strict glare of the Garrison Commander who seemed to conduct them as if they were some sort of military choir. The memory might even have been a good memory if only some of the troops could have sung in tune.

He opened the church door to see the gravedigger filling in the four freshly made graves. That was another puzzle. How had four freshly dug graves appeared in his graveyard? He was sure they weren't there when he arrived this morning. He took off his surplice and pondered on the thought that God really did move in very mysterious circles. He genuflected and forgot all about it.

One the funeral had ended the Commander and his troops began their march across the moorland back to the garrison at Scarborough Castle. Whitby John drove the wagon back to the farmstead. At his side the widow sat dabbing her eyes. In the back Agnes sat quietly with Marmaduke and nine Boggles.

Chapter Fifteen

Once they were all back at the farmhouse Agnes made sure Joan was comfortable and then joined Whitby John and Marmaduke around the large kitchen table. Around them the nine Boggles made themselves comfortable, sitting on the furniture and on the table itself. From nowhere a pot of freshly made coffee and cups appeared. Everyone helped themselves as Agnes held court.

"We have won the battle, but not the war. We have stopped an atrocity happening out there, but our enemy is still at large."

Whitby John cleared his throat. "I've never been too sure of who, or what this enemy is. To be perfectly frank I've no idea of what went on out there on the moor."

That was the cue for the Boggles to tell their story, all at the same time! Agnes slapped her hand on the table. The coffee cups jumped and the Boggles fell silent. The force of her slap was so hard in fact that two of the Boggles fell off the table.

Taking advantage of the silence Agnes told Whitby John of the fight on the moor and the subsequent flight of their enemy. She finished the account by admitting that the man had power and that she had no idea of where he was or what he was liable to do next. Her revelations shut everyone up. A couple of the Boggles glanced anxiously at the farmhouse door.

Agnes smiled. "No he won't come back here. In his eyes his mission has failed. His place of power has been destroyed. Ralphs Cross no longer holds any attractions for him. He's off somewhere else looking for somewhere or something that suits him better. To be honest I'm not even sure whether he will remain in this country."

Whitby John stroked his chin. "There's plenty of old crosses all over the moors. What's to say he just moves to one of them?"

Agnes shook her head. "No there was something about Ralphs Cross. It held some sort of power the others don't have."

She looked up as they all looked back at her. "Don't expect me to explain the whys and wherefores. I just know!"

There was no arguing with Agnes when she used that tone. She clapped her hands.

"Right, time to get back to Scarborough!" She looked across to Whitby John. "If you could stay another day or so it would be useful. Make sure everything's as ship shape as it can be."

Whitby John didn't look happy about staying on, but nodded. "I'll be bankrupt when I get back. The regulars will all be in the Beehive by now. Still family is family. Tell everyone I'll be back in a couple of days."

Agnes smiled. "I think the place will still be standing when you get back." She said.

She looked across to Oggle Boggle. "I am, and always will be, very grateful for your help and for your sacrifice. It is safe for you to return to the moor once more. However should anything occur that you think I should know about, you know where to find me. I never forget a kindness."

As one the Boggles rose from wherever they were seated. Then one at a time, they reached out and with great solemnity they took it turns to shake the hands of Whitby John and Marmaduke. When they approached Agnes each one took a hold of her hand and kissed it on its back. Then silently and in single file they walked out of the back door and off towards the moor.

Agnes then spent some time in private with Joan the farmer's widow before finally calling at the shepherd's cottage to assure the shepherd and his family that everything was safe once more. Then with Marmaduke at her side she returned to Scarborough

Chapter Sixteen

Marmaduke was curled up in the easy chair by the side of the fireplace busy licking his paws after devouring a plate of his favourite sardines. Outside the twenty first century snow was still bring the county to its knees. Agnes sat with a cup of Mr Tetley's finest listening to the drive time radio program. The local reports told her that Scarborough, Filey and Whitby were still isolated due to the snow filled roads. Helicopters had been brought in to help drop food stuff and straw to the cut off villages and livestock. Even the bigger cities like York and Leeds were experiencing difficulties due to the heavy snow. As usual gritting trucks up and down the country had run out of grit and salt and whatever else was needed to spread on the roads. She looked outside into her yard. Her pots of plants and herbs were invisible under the cover of the snow.

She walked through her house and opened her front door. She figured it would be a good idea to show her neighbours that she was still alive and well, if only to dissuade them from calling around with hot soup and concern. A walk down the street to the corner shop would suffice. Once she had made an appearance the whole of the Old Town would know of her state of well-being inside her house. The power cut happened just as she returned to her house. She tutted with annoyance, there were things she had to do and she really didn't need the inconvenience.

She flicked her fingers. The curtains closed, her computer fired up, her kettle boiled and the entire house became bathed in a soft warm glow of candle light, although no candles were burning. By the fireside her one eyed cat snored away.

Time to sit at her computer again. Before she went on-line she skimmed through the information she had downloaded and printed out only a couple of days ago now. She made up three separate piles.

Interesting, rubbish and utter rubbish. The last two piles grew a lot quicker than the first. Eventually she was left with a small pile of papers that held a mention of ancient cults and devil dogs. She read the references once more and waved her fingers at the computer screen.

It wasn't easy to track down but when she eventually discovered it she knew she had found the information she had been searching the internet for. It was the details of a quasi religious sect that dated back beyond the Middle Ages. It seemed to have its roots deep in the forests of Germany and it's basic belief was devil and demon worship. The cult had been driven deep underground by constant attacks from the church. Many of its leaders and followers had been captured and put to death in many creative, cruel and painful methods. Over the years the sect had to curry favour and generate income by the breeding and selling of large hunting dogs that were in demand by courts and royal huntsmen throughout Europe.

As Agnes uncovered more and more about the cult she discovered that the sect, which somehow in the nineteenth century became a "society", a much more genteel name that hid their demonic ambitions and aims. She found that this society existed right through the twentieth century. Then during the First World War they supplied dogs to the German Army. She wasn't surprised to discover they did the same in 1939. In fact the deeper she searched the more she suspected that the "society" wasn't just a supplier to Hitler's Nazi's, but that it was run by a member of the party.

She even uncovered an old photograph of a small band of Nazi party elite posing in the courtyard of an alpine castle. At their feet were two Alsatian dogs. In the background a handler was holding two of the giant black dogs at the end of their leashes. Something about the photograph looked familiar. She looked again and examined the faces in front of her. There it was! In a photograph taken in nineteen forty one was the face of the man in black with red eyes. The very same man she had faced in seventeen seventy nine.

She sat back in her chair. This would take some thinking about. If, what she feared to be true, she had not only come across someone who held great power but someone who seemed to capable of travelling through time.

She considered the dogs. The sect not only used them in their ceremonies, they also bred and sold them to influential people. The dogs had provided the sect with income for centuries. She was unaware of how the creatures were bred but it seemed to have something to do with the earth and its special additives inside the crates. It dawned on her that the man in black seemed to grow the dogs as if they were plants. She smiled. It might have been accidental but Marmaduke had been right to blow up the ones he had discovered. It was just a pity that he destroyed the house and any clues it might have contained.

This called for more help from My Tetley and his miraculous brew. Even after four cups she still didn't have an answer. It might have helped if she could phrase the right question, but there were just too many.

Two things she did know. First, the man in black with red eyes had left the moors and more than likely left Scarborough. Where, she had no idea. She couldn't even be sure if he was in the same time. Secondly she knew he had existed in 1942. Therefore he could be, or had been in the present time. If so had he orchestrated the fate of the Death Metal singer in Finland? It was now obvious to Agnes that the young man had got much further in discovering the existence of the cult and its secrets, much deeper than anyone else. That was why he had to die. She realised the singer himself knew he was in danger. That was why he wrote the lyrics. He wanted someone else to know, he wanted to leave a clue. She thought back. The band member she had spoken to had said it was the last song he recorded, when he had an idea of his own peril. She wondered if there was any unrecorded material in existence.

For a brief moment she considered taking a trip to Finland, then thought better of it. For a start that would mean travelling and Agnes didn't like travelling. Secondly the weather was against her. Even if she could get outside Scarborough all the airports were closed down. Thank goodness for Skype she thought as she made the call.

The young man appeared on the screen. "Hello lady journalist!"

Agnes smiled back. "I need more information." She said and gave him one her very special concentrated looks.

In the background the cat opened his one good eye, looked at the computer and promptly rolled over and went back to sleep.

By the time the conversation had ended Agnes knew a lot more than she ever thought possible about Finnish Death Metal, but more especially about the ill fated singer songwriter.

It seemed the young man had two passions in is short life, music and the occult. At first he was a normal member of the band working hard on his material and his performance, but as his interests in the occult grew so his commitment to the band waned. Although he never missed a performance his attendance at rehearsals grew erratic. At first the rest of the band put it down to the pressures of writing new material. They had recorded their last album only a few weeks before his death and were in the recording studio to approve the final mix and look at new material the singer had written. That interested her. She asked the question and was told what she hoped to hear. The new material had been written around the time of his last recorded song. She asked another question and received the answer she half-expected. The singer had insisted his track about the moors and the dogs be included on the album and that the new material be released as soon as possible. So, she thought, he could have written other songs, to be released later. She asked if any copies of the new material existed. The young man shook his head. Since the singers death no one had listened to any of his new material. Agnes shook her head in frustration. The young man paused and seemed to look around him. He reached off camera and then held up a small memory stick. He told her it had been found in the recording studio. It contained some demos of the singer's rough work. After his death the band had split up and no one had thought to download or listen to it. The young man told her that he would download it and send it to her via her dropbox. Agnes had no idea what a dropbox was but she had a feeling she would soon find out. She was about to thank the young man for his help when he added something as an afterthought. He mentioned that as she was interested in the singers tattoos was she aware he was about to have another one done. It was to fit onto a space on his right calf. He told her it was a drawing of a stone with a strange pattern on it. He had no idea what or where it was. She asked the young man if he could sketch it for her. There was a pause in the conversation whilst he found some paper and a pen. He concentrated. After a few minutes and three bits of screwed up paper he held the paper up to the camera. Agnes waved a finger and her computer took a screen shot of the image. Another wave of her hand and the printer kicked into life. She took the sheet of paper as it emerged from the tray. The young man watched as she examined the print. The man might have been a good musician but he certainly wasn't an artist. Eventually she made sense of it. It was a sketch of a rock and a spiral. It meant nothing to her. The young man then continued the conversation by telling her of his new band and a possible European Tour. She smiled and nodded. The young man finally said goodbye and she watched as he pressed a button. An illuminated button appeared on her screen. It seemed she had a dropbox after all. She spent the rest of the night listening to the demos.

As she listened she realised the difference between a demo and the real thing. The demo was just the singer and his acoustic guitar. She found it interesting and listenable. As she listened the lyrics appeared on the screen in front of her. They seemed to be suitably apocalyptical for the Death Metal genre. It was the fifth track that caught her attention. The song had no title but the main chorus, if two repeated lines constituted a chorus, were about the mask of death creeping out of northern moors. She re-read the lyrics. Another line caught her attention. "At the stone of spiralling cups." She pulled the print of the drawing in front of her. Something about it seemed familiar. There was a feint memory stirring at the back of her mind. She could sit and puzzle herself all night trying to remember, or she could do a Google search, after all the image was already in her computer. She did some finger waving that resulted in a lot of images flashing across her screen until one image settled in the centre of the screen. Despite the lack of artistic talent the photograph on the screen bore a very striking resemblance to the young man's drawing. She pulled up the information and spent the next hour reading everything she could about what archaeologists called "cup and ring" stones.

She discovered they were ancient stone carvings and symbols found throughout Scotland and Northern England. That they were estimated to be between four and five thousand years old, and were usually found by old burial mounds. Others had been found near to stone circles and standing stones. In all cases they seemed to be linked to ancient beliefs and burial practices. Unfortunately they were very common. When she read that over four hundred had been recorded on Ilkley Moor alone she let out a sigh of frustration. She hoped to narrow down the search by identifying the drawing, but all the cup and ring symbols looked the same. The words needle and haystack came to mind. Then she refined her search. The words "cup and ring stones on the North Yorkshire Moors." brought up a lesser number of images. One of them seemed to match her drawing. She checked the reference. It was up on Fylingdales Moors, less than five miles from Ralphs Cross. She had been mistaken. The man in black hadn't left the area. He had just moved his location. Her only problem was, in what time period had the man in black travelled back to.

She waved her hands and the computer shut itself down. That, she thought to herself, was the real magic. Discussion time. She stood up and in one swift movement lifted up her cat, and was down the cellar steps before Marmaduke had time to open his eye.

On the other side of the wall Marmaduke stood blinking his one good eye.

"A bit of warning wouldn't go amiss. Something along the lines of "come with me Marmaduke" would do just as well." He stretched his back in an attempt to get feeling back into his limbs.

"No time – we need to be back up on the moor. Agnes said as she ran up the cellar steps and headed towards the kitchen.

"Now?" exclaimed Marmaduke as he followed her.

As she entered her backyard she turned to him. "I'm not sure if it's now, or then, or sometime in the future, but now will do!"

Chapter Seventeen

Marmaduke never knew how it was done. In fact he didn't want to know. All he remembered was taking on his own cat shape and leaping over walls and hedges and moorland and more moorland. He eventually came to a halt on top of a deserted and very bleak area of moorland. He looked around him. Nothing could be seen in any direction, only moorland and Agnes standing in front of him. She flicked a small brown feather from her shoulder. He watched as it floated to earth, he was sure she only did it for effect. He watched as she stooped and searched among the snow and the heather. She stopped by a small sandy area where the heather had died away. She brushed away the sandy soil and looked up.

"You could help you know!" She remarked.

He gave a shrug. "I would if I knew what you were doing."

She straightened herself and stood with her hands on her hips. "I never was too keen on digging." She stared at the ground very hard. The soil and earth slowly moved to one side revealing a large rock. She took a deep breath and blew. The stone now stood in front of them as clean and as pristine as if it had been polished. On its surface, clearly visible was a carving of a cup and a spiral. She rummaged in her pocket and pulled out the drawing and handed it to Marmaduke. Very quickly she explained her discoveries in her conversation with the young man in Finland. Most of it went completely over his head, but he got the idea. The man in black had either been here, or was going to be here. He blinked his good eye and tried to make sense of it all. In such situations he did what he always did. He checked his two pistols and his knives. Whatever was happening would involve fighting. It always did.

As he checked his weapons Agnes bent down and was examining the rock. She put her hand in her pocket and pulled out some yellow powder.

Carefully she sprinkled it over the stone. At first nothing happened, then very slowly a faint grey smoke drifted up into the cold air. Without warning the smoke began to spark and a small purple flame burst into life. The flames then exploded in a shower of small purple sparks and fell to the floor and died away. Marmaduke looked up from the dying sparks up to Agnes's face. It was set in a very grim expression.

"Something very bad has happened here." She said.

She stepped aside and looked across the moor. Apart from a few distant sheep finding their way through the snow the landscape was deserted. She moved her hands and weaved her fingers into an intricate pattern. Marmaduke turned round. In front of him was a large bell shaped tent. He followed Agnes into its entrance. He wasn't at all surprised to discover that, once inside, he found himself in a very accurate reproduction of their own front room.

"It's just a trick!" Agnes said.

They sat in their comfortable armchairs around their blazing fire. He stretched out and began to close his good eye. She would let him know the whys and wherefores when she knew herself.

Agnes watched as Marmaduke drifted off to sleep. She needed thinking time and moving between the moor and her house was getting tiresome. She pulled her scrying bowl towards her. It was already full of water. She sprinkled some herbs and potions across its surface and watched as the image of the surrounding moorland appeared in front of her. It was mid-morning and the pale sun was trying its best to shine down, causing he snow to sparkle and glimmer. She scanned to the right and to the left. Everything seemed normal. She moved her hand and a vision of the farm appeared. Whitby John and the shepherd were working together chopping wood and piling the logs against the farmhouse wall. In the background the sheep were grazing on the surrounding moor. Life was returning back to normal. Well as normal as it ever could be without the farmer. She moved her hand and the vision disappeared. She put the scrying bowl away and from nowhere a mug of Mr Tetley's finest appeared in her hands.

Thinking time. She pulled out the sheet of paper that held the dead singers lyrics. Well she had found the "stone with the spiralling cups." Now all she had to do was to figure out what the rest of the lyrics to the "Mask of Death from the Northern Moor", meant.

She sat back in her chair and let her mind drift. It found its way over the moor and settled on the stone. Visions appeared. Strange half naked men squatted by the rock. Their bodies were clothed in hides and their skins were tattooed in strange blue patterns. She watched as one of the men carved the intricate pattern on the rocks surface using hard stones and antler horn. She became aware she was watching the birth of the symbol. The men faded away to be replaced by an image of men and women digging. Images of a mound appeared. Then another and another. She saw images of ancient burial rites. Then nothing, just the stone. Always the stone. Then the heather, then as the heather died away the stone again. It became worn, a victim of weathering. The sharpness of the carvings became blurred by the moss and lichens that had grown in its patterns and grooves. Then more heather. Then the stone again. She looked closer. It seemed different. The grooves had been cleaned of moss. The patterns had been picked out in red pigment. She sat up. She had found her man. He was there in the history of the stone. Therefore he was in the past.

She sucked her teeth deep in thought. This was going to take some doing. This was time travel and time travel worried her. The passing between the eighteenth century and the twenty first was easy. That went with the house. All she had to do was walk through the cellar wall. Jumping backwards and forwards across the centuries was a bit more difficult. Very difficult in fact, especially as she hadn't done it before.

It took her the best part of the day and most of the night before she was satisfied she had the right ingredients, the herbs and the potions, aligned with the right spells and incantations. She began casting her spell and a thin, tenuous mist surrounded the outside of the tent.

Marmaduke woke up with a start at the sound of the howling. He leapt to his feet pistols already drawn. He looked at the front of the tent. Agnes was standing by the door looking out. In front of her a large black dog stood its head moving from side to side, sniffing, as if trying to make out what was in front of it. It let out another howl.

Agnes turned to Marmaduke. "It can't see us. It knows something's wrong but it can't work out what."

Sure enough the dog turned and padded back across the moor to join its companions sitting in a large circle, all looking inwards. Looking towards the ancient stone.

Standing over the stone, surrounded by small pots of fire was the man in black. His eyes seemed even redder. As Marmaduke watched the man lifted his hand and a flame appeared over the stone. The pattern danced and echoed among the flames. The dogs all rose to their feet and lifted their heads in one loud blood curdling howl. The flames grew higher and a shape began to appear inside them. It was a shape that, as it made itself clearer, became the parody of a human shape. It turned its head this way and that. It raised its arms and let out a roar. The dogs howled even louder. The man in black with the red eyes raised his arms to the skies and the shape stepped out of the flames.

Agnes raised her arm and pointed her outstretched fingers towards the shape. A beam of silver light flashed across the space and hit the creature full in the chest. It staggered but regained its footing. The man in black turned. He raised his arm and the front of the tent vanished in a purple flash. Agnes moved her hand and the scene changed. Now Marmaduke and Agnes looked out at the man in black in reverse. The tent had relocated behind him. Agnes moved her arm again. The bolt of silver light hit the man in black full in the centre of his back. He stumbled forward. Marmaduke saw his opportunity to attack and ran out of the tent with both pistols drawn. Unfortunately as he left the tent he ran into what he could only assume was an invisible brick wall. He staggered backwards holding his face and nose. He felt blood oozing between his fingers. He looked at Agnes. She pointed a finger and let loose another silver bolt. It flashed across the moor and burst over the landscape. The creature from the flames sensed its approach and raised a hand to catch it. Its hand pulled it from the air and squeezed it. Then with a look of disdain it screwed it up and flung it onto the ground. It sparked once and then died. Agnes shook her head and tried again. This time her bolt shot low across the moorland scorching the heather as it passed by. The man in black turned his head and his eyes flashed the brightest red and the silver bolt exploded in a shower of bright sparks.

As Marmaduke tried to staunch the flow of blood flowing from his nose he watched the creature from the flames. It was changing. It was growing more and more human by the second. Now its appearance was much more human. It was dressed in what appeared to be a series of rags and old bandages giving it the appearance of a very moth eaten, Egyptian mummy. He looked across at Agnes. Her face seemed older, more haggard. Sweat was appearing on her forehead and began to run down her cheeks and face. She moved her hands in an intricate pattern and a web of silver spun from her hands and formed a net over the stone, the man in black and the creature. As the net dropped towards the ground the man in black ducked, rolled and spun around on his feet. As the net fell around him his eyes flashed and the net simply dissolved.

Whilst his concentration was focused on the disappearing net Agnes reached out in front of her. She touched the invisible wall that Marmaduke had run into. Her senses told her it extended all around her tent. With a slight shudder she realised that both her and Marmaduke were trapped inside the tent. She racked her mind to try to find a suitable spell to counteract the man in black's evil magic. As she was thinking she continued to flash bolts of silver threads across the moor. Each thread was negated by the man in black. She realised they were at a stalemate. Beside her Marmaduke kicked the invisible shield in frustration. All he achieved was to hurt his foot.

Both of them realised they were helpless. He glanced across at Agnes. She was busy moving her arms, hands and fingers. The air around them shimmered and glowed. The tent seemed to sway. Marmaduke felt a slight bump. As the movement stopped he looked out of the tent. The scene had changed. The moorland was still outside but there was no sign of the man in black. In the far distance he could just make out a shape. It was the creature now in human shape slowly walking over the moor. He turned to Agnes. She shook her head.

"I moved us a few minutes forward in time. He had us trapped in that tent. It was the only way." Her words came out quickly. Marmaduke frowned. He had never seen Agnes quite like this before. It disturbed him. He looked back across the moor. The creature had now disappeared from view. The landscape was deserted. Agnes sank back in her chair. The inside of the tent returned to the familiarity of her own front room. Marmaduke double checked the entrance to the tent. The landscape had disappeared, so had the entrance. He really was back in his own front room. He knew better than to ask. Anyway it would serve no purpose. Agnes was lost in a very deep sleep. He leant forward and pulled a rug over her. He then stoked the fire up and settled down into his own chair. He didn't sleep, his nose hurt too much.

Chapter Eighteen

"We saw a terrible thing yesterday!"

The comment brought Marmaduke back to the present with a jolt; only he wasn't sure where the present was. He looked down at the leather boots on his feet. He wasn't a cat, therefore he worked out he was at home in the eighteenth century house. He was confused and his nose still hurt. He looked around. Agnes appeared and held out a mug of tea. He took it and cradled it in both hands. Agnes sat in the chair opposite and looked down into her own mug. She spoke without looking up.

"He succeeded. He actually raised a demon."

Marmaduke didn't know what to say, so he said nothing.

"We can only be thankful he didn't raise it here and now." She paused and looked thoughtful.

"I'm not too sure I could have stopped it had he succeeded."

Marmaduke gave a slight couch. Agnes looked up at him.

"Go on, ask away!"

"What was that thing?"

Agnes sat back in her chair. "It was a terrible thing. It was a demon."

Marmaduke scratched the back of his head trying to find the right words, phrase the right question. Eventually he leant forward.

"It looked like demon when it first appeared. Then it seemed to morph into a human shape before changing into something that looked, well, looked rotten!"

"Putrification. Those weren't bandages, they were the remains of a burial shroud that had rotted away."

"So what happened next? Did it just wander off and rot away somewhere on the moor?"

Agnes shook her head and took a deep gulp of tea. Then she placed the mug on her lap, holding it tight between her hands. She looked Marmaduke straight in the eye.

"If only it was that simple. No it was a demon. A particularly nasty and evil demon. It was the demon of pestilence."

Marmaduke looked puzzled. Agnes continued her explanation. "I managed to get us back in time, you know. I didn't think I could do that with such accuracy. Unfortunately I didn't get the spell quite right. We sort of got there, but we couldn't get out of the tent."

Marmaduke instinctively felt his nose. Agnes continued talking.

"In fact the more I think about it, the more I'm not too sure whether we actually were there or we just formed some sort of portal. Actually I've no idea what I did. Our magic could pass through the tent doorway, we couldn't."

Marmaduke scratched his head once more. No matter how hard he tried he just couldn't understand the whole magic time travel thing. All he really knew was that he was transported across distances of miles and years in what seemed like the blink of an eye. He didn't want to know how, or why it happened. All he knew was that usually it didn't hurt and that there was usually a fight at the other end.

"What about the man in black?" he asked.

Agnes shook her head. "Our man in black has gone. He's not dead, far from it. No doubt he is somewhere in time. Somewhere breeding his devil dogs, somewhere attempting to raise demons, somewhere, sometime causing as much death and destruction as possible."

A frown crossed Marmaduke's brow. He changed over hands and continued to scratch his head.

"You don't get it do you?" before he could answer she shook her head and continued. "No, and there's no reason you should. Somehow I followed our man in black backwards through time, all the way back to 1348 in fact."

Marmaduke's face remained blank. Agnes continued her explanation. "That was the year of the Great Plague. Someone once estimated that over one and a half million people out of a population of four million died in the next two years. The creature that the man in black called into being was the demon of disease."

Marmaduke sank back in his chair as the enormity of what he had just heard sank in. In fact he spent a long time working out the various ramifications. When he came to take a sip of his tea it had gone cold.

"Let me get this straight in my head." He began. "The man in black is a time travelling, demon raiser, hell bent on creating as much death and damage as possible. Why?"

Agnes moved her fingers and suddenly Marmaduke found himself holding a hot cup of tea.

"Yes that's precisely what he is. Him and his assistant. As to why, I have no idea. I suspect there will be a reason. I suspect the man in black is just an instrument of some cult, or a cabal, or some people who are working to some sort of plan"

She clapped her hands on her knees. "To be honest I don't really know and I don't really want to know. It's not my role in life to go chasing through time and goodness knows where after the likes of him. He's someone else's problem now. I did what I had to do and, looking back, I'm pretty pleased with myself."

"And what did you have to do" Asked Marmaduke. He suspected he knew the answer, but Agnes had expected him to feed her the line and he didn't want to disappoint her.

Agnes smiled. "My role is to look after Scarborough, and its people, and I think I achieved that rather well."

Chapter Nineteen

The following morning Agnes and Marmaduke made their way down to the Three Mariners to welcome Whitby John home. It seemed as if half the Old Town had come up with the same idea. The small inn was surrounded by the fishermen and their wives and their children who didn't really know what was going on. But an occasion was an occasion and they had no intention of missing out.

As they saw Marmaduke and Agnes approach the crowd parted to make a corridor straight to the door of the inn. As she entered the door Agnes paused and looked around. It was the first time she had ever seen the full interior of the bar. Instead of the dingy, smoke filled pit of gloom there was light and brightness and sparkle and cleanliness and colour. Curtains hung down both sides of brightly polished windows through which the sun shone. It sparkled and glistened among the polished tankards and bottles and glasses. It enhanced the colours of the sprays of flowers placed in small vases at the centre of each table. It was the first time she had ever seen the floorboards. Usually they were covered in damp, beer sodden rushes and sawdust. Today they shone with polish.

Sat in their usual seats Salmon Martin, Old Sam and Martin Tong raised their shiny pewter tankards towards her. She pushed her way across the room and joined them in her usual seat. She had hardly settled down when Baccy Lad appeared with a tankard of ale for her. She sniffed it. It smelt fresh and inviting. She took a drink and bust into a cough. She hadn't sniffed the double gin in it. She looked across to the bar where Mrs Pateley stood. She looked up from serving and gave Agnes a broad smile and a wink. As she served Agnes noticed that the people wanting a drink had actually formed an orderly queue around the bar. That was another first.

The door opened. Everyone stopped speaking and drinking and looked at the figure that stood on the threshold. The figure didn't move for a few seconds. It just stood there opening and closing its mouth as its head moved from side to side trying to take everything in. At one point, (Agnes thought it was when he noticed the curtains, she had her doubts about them herself. Much too floral for her liking) his eyes almost seemed to pop out of his head. Before he could say anything a female voice echoed across the bar room.

"Welcome home Whitby John!"

It took three strides for John to move behind the bar. Then before anyone, especially the widow Pateley, could say anything, he swept her up in both of his arms and held her close to him. Everyone held their breath as he leant forward and kissed her. Someone tried to cheer, until he caught Agnes looking at him. Without a word to each other, or to the customers the couple linked hands and walked off to the private area behind the bar. As the door shut behind them the occupants of the bar burst into a tidal wave of cheers and conversation. Tankards were lifted, glasses chinked, bottles were opened. Baccy Lad was run off his feet. Agnes gave a slight nod to Marmaduke. They slipped out into the street.

"I suppose I'll be after getting a new hat!" She said.

Three Months Later

The roads were clear. The winter had passed into spring. The trees were in bud. On the seafront the arcades, amusements and pleasure boats were getting their spring spruce ups. Everything smelt of fresh paint. Everyone was preparing for the coming summer season. At the railway station a mixture of day visitors rubbed shoulders with business people and other travellers. Among them was an elderly lady pulling a small overnight case on wheels behind her. The people who left the train from York walked out into the street where cars waited for visiting family members. Taxis waited for anyone who could afford one. Holiday makers dragged their cases and luggage towards their hotels and boarding houses.

Agnes pulled her case on wheels out of the station, across the pedestrian crossing that turned to a green man as she approached and she headed down Westborough towards the old Town and home. It had been a good trip but it was always nice to be back home. Anyway she had only been away three nights. She shook her head slightly. The roaring noise in her ears was beginning to fade away. Well what do you expect if you have just spent two days at a Death Metal Festival? Still it had been worth it. She found she actually liked some of the bands. She doubted the dress sense of many of them but on the whole they were a decent lot, especially the new Finnish death metal band. She had spent a lot of time with them backstage, and later at their hotel. It had been good to speak to the young man face to face. This time she had told him the full story, which he then insisted she retold to the rest of the band and their road crew. All of them knew Tapio and all of them in some way had been affected by his sudden death.

At least they have closure she thought as she opened her front door. Her cat lifted its head from its spot sunning itself on top of the green wheelie bin. It heard movement in the kitchen and went to investigate; Agnes was back, there just might be sardines for tea.

END.

ABOUT THE AUTHOR

Graham Rhodes has over 40 years experience in writing scripts, plays, books, articles, and creative outlines. He has created concepts and scripts for broadcast television, audio-visual presentations, computer games, film & video productions, web sites, audio-tape, interactive laser-disc, CD-ROM, animations, conferences, multi-media presentations and theatres. He has created specialised scripts for major corporate clients such as Coca Cola, British Aerospace, British Rail, The Co-operative Bank, Bass, Yorkshire Water, York City Council, Provident Finance, Yorkshire Forward, among many others. His knowledge of history helped in the creation of heritage based programs seen in museums and visitor centres throughout the country. They include The Merseyside Museum, The Jorvik Viking Centre, The Scottish Museum of Antiquities, & The Bar Convent Museum of Church History.

He has written scripts for two broadcast television documentaries, a Yorkshire Television religious series and a Beatrix Potter Documentary for Chameleon Films and has written three film scripts, The Rebel Buccaneer, William and Harold 1066, and Rescue (A story of the Whitby Lifeboat) all currently looking for an interested party.

His stage plays have performed in small venues and pubs throughout Yorkshire. "Rambling Boy" was staged at Newcastle's Live Theatre in 2003, starring Newcastle musician Martin Stephenson, whilst "Chasing the Hard-Backed, Black Beetle." won the best drama award at the Northern Stage of the All England Theatre Festival and was performed at the Ilkley Literature Festival. Other work has received staged readings at The West Yorkshire Playhouse, been short listed at the Drama Association of Wales, and at the Liverpool Lesbian and Gay Film Festival.

He also wrote dialogue and story lines for THQ, one of America's biggest games companies, for "X-Beyond the Frontier" and "Yager" both winners of European Game of the Year Awards, and wrote the dialogue for Alan Hanson's Football Game (Codemasters) and many others.

OTHER BOOKS BY GRAHAM RHODES

"Footprints in the Mud of Time, The Alternative Story of York"

"More Poems about Sex 'n Drugs & Rock 'n Roll & Some Other Stuff

"The York Sketch Book." (a book of his drawings)

"The Jazz Detective."

The Agnes the Witch Series

"A Witch, Her Cat and a Pirate."

"A Witch, Her Cat and the Ship Wreckers."

"A Witch, Her Cat and the Demon Dogs"

Photographic Books

"A Visual History of York." (Book of photographs)

"Leeds Visible History" (A Book of Photographs)

"Harbourside - Scarborough Harbour
(A book of photographs available via Blurb)

"Lost Bicycles."
(A book of photographs of deserted and lost bicycles available via Blurb)

"Trains of the North Yorkshire Moors."
(A Book of photographs of the engines of the NYMR available via Blurb

Made in the USA
Charleston, SC
28 February 2017